The One to Heal

BOOK ONE

ROSE RIDGE

RANCH

LIZ LOVELOCK

Cover Design by Ben Ellis from Tall Story
Edited by Lauren from Creating Ink
Nikki and Kaylene from Swish Design and Editing
Proofread by Lisa Vincent
Formatted by Tami at Integrity Formatting

www.lizlovelockauthor.com

The One to Heal

to

BOOK ONE

ROSE RIDGE RANCH

Liz Lovelock

Chapter 1

Sebastian

QUICKLY, I RUN THROUGH THE hospital door and head straight for the reception desk.

I want answers.

I want to know where my wife is.

As I stride past the few people lined up, they give me filthy glares. The desk is empty as the nurse finishes some paperwork before calling the next person. I get to the white-haired lady, slapping my hands on the desk. "Where are my wife and daughter, Anna-Beth and Rylee King? They were in a car accident. My wife is p-pregnant." My voice cracks on the last word.

One of my closest friends, Reuben, comes up beside me, his eyes full of panic. I'm sure they match mine.

"I'm sorry, sir. You'll need to take a seat while I find out what I can for you. Please give me a moment, and I'll be right back." She turns to a younger nurse standing close by and says something I don't hear. They swap places, and the white-haired lady walks out of the area. How am I supposed to sit and wait for news?

"It'll be all right, Seb. Come on." Reuben grips my arm and pulls me away toward some empty chairs in the waiting area. I let him lead me, but my eyes stay trained on the white-haired lady as she walks through a set of doors.

The fight Anna-Beth and I had this morning replays in my head. Oh heck! I grab Reuben's shoulder to steady myself. "Reuben, we got into a stupid argument this morning, and I left before we settled it. What if I don't get the chance t-to fix things with her?" Tears fill my eyes, threatening to fall.

Reuben pulls me in for a hug. He's the brother I never got, and I don't know what I would do without him right now.

"Don't think like that," he says.

"I need to know what's going on, Reuben. I need to see Anna-Beth."

"I know. I'm sure they won't keep you waiting. Let's take a seat." He sits in the chair behind him, and I follow suit. The world is spinning around me. I want it to stop, and I want to be with my wife and Rylee. I *need* them both to be okay. I can't do life without either of them.

"They need to be okay, Reuben." I drop my face into my hands. My heart is pounding, and I'm unable to settle its fast rate.

The last thing I should have done was walk out. But my job took priority, and I left. The desire to become a Formula One world champion overrides my family's needs yet again.

She stood in our bedroom doorway, her hand resting on her swollen belly. The light pink flowing dress she was wearing made her glow.

"I don't have time for this right now. I have to go," I snapped at Anna-Beth. My tone was harsh even to my own ears, and her eyes went wide as though I'd physically slapped her.

We never argued like that. Of course, married couples have disagreements, but this was different.

That look in her eyes…

The hurt was evident in the tears that pooled.

She turned her back on me without another word and walked away.

"Gee, she looks like she needs to be back in a hospital bed," Reuben says, pulling me back into my present nightmare.

I glance up and look around to see what's caught his attention. A young woman who's clutching at her stomach. The frail blonde-haired woman takes tiny steps, stumbling slightly, her face set and she bites her lip as she makes her way through the emergency waiting area.

"She looks to be in pain, but she's not stopping," Reuben says, our focus now on the woman in front of us.

With my attention on her, I wait to see what she's doing. "Yeah, she doesn't look good."

Should I help?

If it were Anna-Beth, I'd want someone to help her. I rise from my seat and take a step toward her, but as I do, her legs crumble beneath her. Rushing to her side, I scoop her up in my arms, dropping to my knees before her head hits the floor.

"Are you okay?" Her head rolls and rests against my chest. Turning to the desk, I call, "Help, she's collapsed."

"I'm fine," she grinds out breathlessly. "I need to get to my baby. I want to see her." She sobs. I assist her into a sitting position, and she hisses with the movement.

Her blonde, matted hair covers her face, and she reaches up, pushing it aside. Her piercing blue eyes meet mine, and tears stream down her rose-pink cheeks.

"You're in the wrong place. This is the emergency room. Your baby would be upstairs in the maternity or pediatric ward. I can help you get to her, but it looks like you need some medical attention first. The nurses will bring your baby to you... just ask them," I say softly, trying to reassure her as her body trembles under my touch.

Her hair moves as she shakes her head. "Not when *he's* there. He won't let me see her. I haven't even held her." She folds into herself and clutches her arms around her stomach. I hold her tightly against me, rubbing her back and offering some comfort.

"Move aside, sir, so we can help her."

My body spins around to the voice that belongs to the nurse from the desk. She glances behind her to the two other nurses standing by. "Could you assist me with getting her in the wheelchair please?" They come forward, and I maneuver her in a way that makes it easier for them to help.

"She wants to see her baby," I say.

"I'll take care of it as soon as she's been seen by the doctor," the nurse says as the other two scoop her gently from my arms and place her in the chair with care.

"Get your hands off my wife," a cold voice says from behind me. A heavy hand lands on my shoulder. I twist, shrugging it off, glaring into the guy's dark eyes as he sneers at me, then back to the young woman in the chair.

Her body goes rigid—it's clear she's scared of him

Is this the *he* she was referring to?

Sizing him up, I take in his forced smile and pause at his well-kept appearance. His hands clench, then release. Uncaring. Unkind. There's no mistaking why the woman fears him.

"She collapsed, and I caught her before she hit the floor." I swallow the slew of words I want to unleash on this man. No concern or care for his wife or the state she's in, only that I was touching her. She isn't his first care. He should have at least asked if she was okay.

The unkind man turns to his wife, getting down and into her face. She won't meet his eyes. "What are you doing, Delilah?" he asks through gritted teeth, almost sounding like a snake's hiss.

"I… I wanted to see Olive, Eli, she needs her mom. I need to see her. Please, Eli," she replies breathlessly.

Eli ignores Delilah's plea and straightens, turning his pinched expression back on me. "She's fine," he replies in a tone that would send a shiver down anyone's spine.

"Okay. She just appeared to need some help, so that's what I did. Next time, how about you take care of her instead of worrying about me," I snap, unable to hold my tongue. Eli's fiery glare focuses firmly on me.

Reuben takes a step in front of me. "Eli, is it? Look… she needed help and my friend here offered it. She collapsed. We'll leave you to look after *your* family."

Before Eli has a chance to respond, my name is called from behind.

"Excuse me, Mr. King," someone says.

I turn away from Eli to find a doctor, instantly

forgetting the man but not the woman's fearful stare. I blink and turn my focus back to my family. "How are my wife, daughter, and baby?" I ask the doctor. Reuben is at my side within seconds. I need his support.

"Your daughter, Rylee, is in a stable condition and has come away unharmed aside from a few bruises and scrapes. She'll be sore, though it's nothing pain medication can't fix." He falls silent and glances down at the folder he's clutching.

Relief washes over me before meeting his gaze again. "And my wife?" Fear laces through me like little tendrils wrapping around my chest, squeezing—stealing my breath.

"I'm so sorry, Mr. King, but your wife is in a critical condition." He pauses, and with the thundering of my heartbeat flooding my ears, I'm not sure I've heard him correctly.

"What did you say?" I choke.

The doctor clears his throat and then says, "Unfortunately, your wife, Anna-Beth, suffered severe head injuries, and because of those injuries, she's unresponsive and will not wake. We are closely monitoring her for the baby's sake, and at this time, we think it's best to deliver the baby now." He stands in front of me in his dark blue scrubs, his mouth continues to move, but I can't hear anything he's saying.

Unresponsive.

Deliver.

Baby.

Now.

Someone gently touches my elbow.

I shake my head, bringing the new world that's been laid out in front of me into focus. "I'm sorry, what... what does that mean, non-responsive?" The lump in my throat catches, the words struggling to come out, and I swallow. An arm slips around my shoulders, yet I still stand there, unsure of what to do. How do I proceed without the love of my life?

The doctor shuffles on his feet before saying, "What it means, Mr. King, is that your wife won't regain consciousness and is currently on life support. It's imperative that the baby is delivered as soon as possible. I'm terribly sorry..."

"Seb, I'm so sorry. Did you hear? They're delivering the baby. I'm sorry about Anna-Beth," Reuben says beside me. I shift my eyes to meet his. Tears are sliding down his face. I shut mine for a moment and nod. I clench them tightly, attempting to soothe the burning sensation but only causing my own tears to form and drop like raindrops down my cheeks.

"So, you're telling me there's no chance my wife is going to wake up again?" It's as though my chest is tearing open with each word spoken. The raw pain is unfathomable and unfixable — an open wound that has no timeframe for healing.

The doctor hangs his head then glances up.

The grim expression etched into his face is one I don't think I'll ever erase from my mind. I'll remember him always—he's given me the worst news of my life. "No, she won't, but we have a plan to save the baby. Our obstetrician is with your wife right now, and the baby will be here any moment, and then if you like, you can see your wife. Is your wife an organ donor, Mr. King?"

The baby is okay, but my wife isn't.

My beautiful Anna-Beth, the most kindhearted woman in my life… is gone. She was my number-one supporter, biggest fan and always helped me in my career, took wonderful care of our little girl, and was growing another to add to our crew.

The wound in my chest opens more. My hand clutches at my shirt as my legs grow weak. My breaths are short, and with each one, it becomes harder to breathe. The world around me keeps moving—nurses, family, people entering and leaving the hospital—but I can't take my girl home. My legs buckle beneath me. The mere thought of seeing her in that state frightens me, but I do want to see her one last time.

Reuben's grip around my arms tightens as he lowers me into the seat I'd just been sitting in before the woman collapsed in front of me. "I got you, man."

"I'm sorry, sir, but we need an answer on the

organ donation as we will need to organize UNOS and sometimes, in these cases, organs will only be viable for a limited amount of time," the doctor urges me again. I know he's trying to be supportive but punching him would feel good right about now. That's my wife he's talking about wanting to cut up.

"Just give him a minute to process things." I hear Reuben say as I lose myself in my thoughts once again.

Anna-Beth and I had quite a few conversations about death. As a Formula One race car driver, I've always been aware of my mortality. We spoke about what would occur if something happened to me, and I was non-responsive, and I told her to give away my organs. Her response was a kiss on the lips, and she'd said, *"As hard as it would be for me to let any part of you go to a stranger, I know they'd need it more. So, if something ever happens to me, give my organs as well."*

"Um… yes, she's a donor and I'd really like to see her," I pause and then say, "Will… will she be attached to machines?"

The doctor places his hand on my shoulder and squeezes. "Yes, she will until we're prepared for the procedure and other hospitals will be informed by UNOS. I'm truly sorry for your loss, Mr. King. I'll be back shortly, and I'll have some paperwork for you to fill out, then you can go to your daughter, and we'll bring your baby to you when it's born. We'll give you some time and then come get you after we're done for you to see your wife. Again, I'm truly sorry for your loss."

I can't look up at him again—his face only brings pain. He's the bearer of bad news, but it's not his fault. I should've been with her. Instead, I was at a training session, trying to get more time on the simulator. This year was supposed to be my world championship year. This was it, and now it's all vanished—the love of my life, my rock, is no longer here.

Guilt claws at my insides. She'd wanted me to spend the day with Rylee and her before the baby came in three weeks. And now… she's gone, and I can't take back the words I said to her. We'd had a stupid little fight—that was the last conversation we'd had. I didn't mean to lose my cool, but she always understood that the world championship was my goal, even before we were married. And now Rylee is four years old, and things changed again. Still, Anna-Beth supported me, a wave of nausea rolls through me.

The nurse comes back with a clipboard full of paperwork. "Where's my daughter? Rylee King?" I ask her.

"She's down the hall in room eight. Her grandmother is with her. Please complete these forms and then you can go to her."

"Grandmother?" I ask, my brows furrow. *I didn't ring Mom.*

"I rang her before we left the track and told her

to come," Reuben says as though he's read my mind.

"I rub my forehead. "Oh... right. Thank you." I'm glad we added her as an emergency contact, or they wouldn't have let her through.

The nurse hands the folder to me, and the urge to run down the hall to Rylee surges through me. *She's with Mom*, I remind myself and attempt to settle the thumping in my chest. I take a moment to do the paperwork. Reuben takes it back to the counter and then returns to my side. I need to see Rylee.

"She's okay," Reuben assures me as if reading my mind. "They've checked her over, and she's got some bumps and bruises. Let's go see her." I nod.

I need to see my daughter.

To hold her.

Reuben helps me up and throws his arm over my shoulders, leading me down the hall. People walk by us, their lives not turned upside down like mine is now. I'm sure they have their own issues going on, but the loss of Anna-Beth will be hard to heal from — if one can heal from it. I don't think I'll ever recover.

We stop in front of a closed cream-colored door with an eight lit up above it. Reuben gives me a reassuring glance before releasing me and pushing it open. I step into the sterile-smelling room and stop when I see my little girl lying on the bed, her grandmother, my mom, with her. Mom's holding Rylee's tiny hand in her big, comforting one. My mom glances up as we enter, and her eyes fill with tears when she sees my face.

"Gran, what's wrong?" Rylee's sweet voice is a knife into my heart and a massive relief at the same time. Thank goodness she's okay, but how do I even begin to tell her about her mom?

Rylee rolls over in the bed and faces me. A little red bump on her head stands out. "Daddy!" Her outstretched arms wait for me, and I rush into them. I clutch her against my chest as waves of hurt, love, and strength crash into me.

"Oh, baby, how are you feeling?" I say into her hair as I inhale the familiar lavender shampoo scent—the same one Anna-Beth uses. My eyes sting with tears, and I can't stop them. I hold Rylee tighter, lifting and placing her in my lap, sitting on the bed. Small sobs fill the room, and I realize they're coming from me.

"Daddy? What's wrong?" Rylee pulls back and stares at me. Her little hand comes up and wipes away the wetness on my cheeks. "Why you sad?"

I take in a deep breath. This is a conversation I never wanted to have with one of my kids.

Rylee's sweet blue eyes gaze into mine. They're her mother's blue eyes. She's her mother's mini, except for the hair that's almost black like mine. "Baby, it's about Mommy and the car accident." My voice cracks, and my body trembles. I hold her tighter to me.

"Where's Mommy?" She turns her head around the room and is met with Reuben and her gran. Not her mother. The one person she probably wants. Whenever she's gotten hurt in the past, she's always run to Anna-Beth, even if I was right beside her, and Anna-Beth started comforting her first. She's always had a special bond with her mom.

"Mommy got badly hurt in the car accident, and she's…" I scrunch my eyes closed and take a breath before continuing, "She's gone to live with Grandpop in heaven."

Rylee is silent for a moment and then snuggles into me more. "We won't see mom again?"

Her sadness ripples through me, and I wish I could take away the hurt and pain she's experiencing in this moment. She's going to grow up without her mom. She won't have her mother with her on her wedding day or when she has kids of her own. It's all on me now. I have to be there for her.

"No, baby, we won't see her again, but we can always talk to her, and you've got your baby sister coming today." I attempt strength, but the sob from Mom causes fresh tears in my own eyes. Looking up, I see Reuben has her in his arms. I'd be lost without his support today.

"I'm going to miss her." Rylee sobs into my

black shirt, the material soaking up the tears as I tighten my grip and gently rub her back.

"She was mine too… mine too." Sadness and sorrow ripple through the room. How are we ever going to find happiness again amongst so much darkness?

A light knock at the door draws all our attention. I don't move from my spot, though. My little girl needs me, and I'm not going anywhere.

Reuben releases Mom and goes to the door, pulling it open and a nurse walks in pushing a baby crib. Inside is a little bundle wrapped in a pink hospital blanket. Ruby. That was the name Anna-Beth had chosen. We hadn't agreed, but it's what she wanted, and that's the name our child will get.

"Mr. King, meet your daughter." The nurse lifts the pink bundle from the cot, brings her to me, and gently places her in my free arm with Rylee watching closely in my other.

"This is my sister?" She doesn't look away from Ruby's chubby, light pink face. Rylee's was the same.

"Yes, she's beautiful. Her name is Ruby."

Mom comes over and takes Rylee from my lap, and I fully take in this little angel. She didn't come into the world the way we'd planned. Sometimes we're given these hardships, but this is a new level of life I will have to wade through.

Leaning down, I press my lips to Ruby's

forehead. She squirms a little, and her tiny cries make my heart race. "Shh… it's okay. I've got you," I whisper, planting another kiss on her head. "Come meet your sister, Ry."

Rylee walks over with a big smile on her face—her mother's. "She is cute." She gently rubs Ruby's head and plants a kiss in almost the same spot I did.

My new world.

Not the world I wanted, but this is how it is now.

My sweet Anna-Beth is gone. My heart is broken, and I'm not sure how to move forward. I'm sure these two little girls will be able to teach me what I need to do.

After about twenty minutes a knock at the door draws my attention. Glancing up from Ruby sleeping in my arms, the desire to hold both my girls tightly and never let them go tugs at my heart. Rylee lays in the bed with mom. I stand from my seat.

"Mr. King, your wife is ready, if you would like to see her." Her words catch in her throat, but then she clears it away and waits for my answer.

A lump forms in my throat—I'm not ready to say goodbye.

"Ah, yeah, okay. Mom?" I glance down at Ruby in my arms and Mom rises from the bed and takes her from me. My eyes drop to Rylee who lies there asleep. I hope her dreams are of her mom and nothing bad from the accident.

Mom places a kiss on my cheek. "Give her my love. I'll watch the girls."

"I'll stay here too," Reuben offers and moves to stand beside mom, wrapping his arm around her shoulders.

"Okay," I respond breathlessly. Turning to the nurse I say, "Take me to her, please."

With a heavy heart I follow her out of the room and down a corridor then into an elevator. I'm sure my heart could drop us to the ground with the weight it's carrying. No one should have to say goodbye to the love of their life at such a young age, it's wrong.

The elevator dings and the doors open. No words are spoken between us, and I really have nothing to say to the nurse or anyone else, I just want to see Anna-Beth.

Finally, she stops at the door. "She's inside. I'll make sure no one disturbs you."

"Thank you." I swallow the lump and grip my hands together in front of me then release them and grip the door handle, pushing down it clicks, and I push it open.

I stop in my tracks, sucking in a breath. Releasing the door, I rush to Anna-Beth's bedside. Hoping, wishing she'd open her eyes. She looks as though she's asleep but the beep of machines and the breathing machine in operation lassoes around my chest and tugs me right back into my reality. Her eyes remain closed as I gently take her hand.

The dam of emotions I'd been keeping at bay rush through me, so I drop to my knees, my head resting on our hands. Each sob ripping right through me, opening a new wound every single time. "I'm so sorry," I whisper while tasting fresh salty tears. "I'm so sorry for everything. Ruby is beautiful." I hiccup then inhale a deep breath.

"I wish you would wake up that this was all just a bad dream. I need you here to help me with the girls. They need their momma and I need you." I drag a hand down my face but never let her go. Rising on wobbly legs, I study her face, wanting to remember every single detail of her. Her usual pink cheeks and lips are now dull. I'll never look into those beautiful eyes again. Hear her familiar sweet voice or have her fill a room with laughter.

Leaning over I place a kiss on each cheek, one on the forehead and one on her lips. "I love you, Anna-Beth, and I always will. You are the mother of our daughters and the love of my life. You're going to live on in other people and give them life. You were always so thoughtful and giving." Fresh tears drop and land on the sheets.

I take a seat and stay with her until a gentle knock comes. Dread pools within my stomach,

I'm not ready. My body trembles as the door opens. Reuben steps in, his face crumbles the moment his eye land on Anna-Beth. But he's not alone. The same doctor from the emergency room also enters.

"Mr. King, I'm sorry. It's time. Would you like to walk with her?"

I nod, not wanting to let go of her hand just yet. Reuben comes and stands beside me, tears glistening on his cheeks.

The doctor turns and says something in a hushed tone, then a group of nurses come in and do I don't even know what, but then we are walking out the door. Down a small corridor that soon opens into a wider one.

I inhale a sharp breath when I see the corridor lined with hospital workers. Uncontrollable sobs pour from me. Reuben steadies me as we walk to the looming doors that I can't pass through.

The bed comes to a stop.

I turn to Anna-Beth, my love.

Leaning over, I place one last kiss on her soft lips. "I love you. Forever. Goodbye, beautiful."

Chapter 2

Delilah

Eleven Months Later

As I DRIVE DOWN THE winding road, the main house comes into focus—its brick exterior with slightly faded white beams on the patio. Large, neatly trimmed hedges surround it. I swallow the lump forming in my throat. I can't believe I'm finally back here. The smell, this place, the memories begin to swallow me. I push them aside for now and focus on pulling up and getting out of the car when the time comes.

Am I going to be welcomed back, or will they all still hate me for what I did?

Coming up to the final stretch of the long driveway, I head up a slight incline. People are roaming around the ranch with wide and vibrant smiles lighting up their faces. Bodies move from one stable to another, some carrying bales of hay and others leading horses from a trailer. My body trembles and overwhelming fear takes hold of my chest. *Keep going. Keep going. The hardest part is nearly over.*

All eyes turn to me as I drive slowly past everyone. I can't bring myself to stare back. My aim is to get to the homestead and hopefully be allowed to stay.

Finally, I pull up at the house and kill the engine. Before I can even contemplate getting out of the car, my door flies open, and I stare into the hazel eyes of Hudson, my oldest and super-protective brother.

"Delilah?" There's shock in the word.

"Hey, Hudson." I unbuckle my belt and climb from my car. He moves back. His wide eyes travel up and down my body.

"Get in here." Before I can protest, he takes my arm and pulls me against him. His familiar scent of pine, hay, and horse brings a smile to my face. "It's so good to see you again. It's been too long."

"At least someone is happy to see me," I mutter as I pull away from his embrace and stare up at him. He's aged well over the years. "What's with this?" I reach up and rub my palm over the stubble he has growing.

He chuckles. "Hey, I look rugged and handsome, according to Odette."

"She likes to build up your ego any way she can."

"Come on. Let's get you settled. What's brought you home?" he hesitantly asks.

"Isn't Dad unwell? That's the information I got."

Hudson's brow furrows as those familiar eyes take me in. "Dad's fine. Who's giving you that information?"

"Damn, Isla," I mutter.

Hudson laughs, nudging me on the shoulder. "She got you good."

I think back to my last conversation with Isla when she gave me this misinformation. Deep down, I felt as though she might have been lying to me. That's where Olive is right now—with Isla—and boy, do I miss my little sidekick. I guess my breakdown a week ago forced her into this lie.

"No, I think she knew what I needed. To finally come home," I say thoughtfully.

Hudson is silent for a beat, wraps his arm around my shoulder, and tugs me against his side. "Welcome back to Rose Ridge Ranch, sis. You're home."

Chapter 3

Delilah

Tears sting my eyes. It's been too long. Turning in a circle, I take in the full scope of the property, the lush green hills and tall trees. In the distance on the far hill, I spot the old house, the white exterior with overgrown bushes surrounding it. My chest squeezes when I think about my times with Eli in that house.

"Dee…"

As I spin around, I see Odette is doing her best, running toward me. I catch her. Her arms tighten around me, and this time, I can't stop the tears. They fall freely. I've missed her sweet spirit.

"Hey, baby sister." We stay like this for a moment before she finally releases me.

"Good see you," she stumbles over her

words — her speech impediment has always been a challenge for her. But she's come so far, and no disability will hold her back.

I hold her out at arm's length and study her. Her dark hair is plaited in pigtails with red ribbons tied on the ends. Freckles are lightly sprayed on her nose and cheeks, and her excited blue eyes stare at me.

"It's so good to see you as well. I've missed you." I swipe a tear from my already wet cheek.

"I miss… you too." Her eyes shut and clench as she tries to get the right words out. "You… stay?"

"I'm staying for as long as I'm allowed."

Odette throws her arms in the air and spins in a circle, her head turned up toward the sky — *her happy dance*. I've missed seeing this girl. She always manages to bring a smile to my face.

I laugh, and the happiness that flows through me because of this simple moment steals my breath. I haven't felt this light in a long time.

"Come. You m-meet Devon, m-my boyfriend."

I glance over my shoulder and shoot a questioning look at Hudson.

"Yeah, her boyfriend. He's been working here almost a year, and he's a cool kid. His sister is married to the basketball player, Parker Kent."

My mouth drops. "You're joking, right?"

Odette takes my hand and leads me away from Hudson, who follows us.

He shakes his head. "No, no joke. He was having trouble with college and fitting in as he's got special needs as well. Addison, his sister, and Parker came to stay for a holiday and realized what we did here. The next time, they showed up out of the blue and brought Devon with them, and he hasn't left."

"*Parker Kent's* brother-in-law works and lives here?" I ask, unable to hide my shock. I'm a massive sports buff. Basketball and Formula One are my ultimate favorites.

"Yeah. Devon and Odette clicked right away and became close friends. It was actually pretty cute. They're both smart kids."

"Wow, I've missed so much. I wonder why Sybil didn't tell me when we spoke and messaged each other."

Hudson shrugs. "That's something you'd have to ask her."

Odette continues to pull me along as we head down to the largest and oldest big red barn. It's been here the longest—so long the red has faded to a brown and is peeling in places.

"Why did you never try to contact me?" I ask Hudson. Even though he gave me the warmest welcome I could've asked for, he was one of the reasons I left in the first place.

Hudson drags a hand down his face and sighs.

"I'm sorry, Dee. I guess…" he pauses for a second and then continues, "…I didn't think you'd want to talk to me. I'd said some hurtful things, and I suppose they were probably unforgivable…" I'm taken straight back to that night he's referring to. He told me I was stupid and said I was making the biggest mistake of my life. If only I could tell him he was right. Maybe one day I will when my pride isn't hurting so much.

"I don't think I'd have wanted to talk to you if I'm being honest. I've been angry for a long time. It's only been in this last year that I think I've needed my family… needed to mend those broken parts of our home."

Hud's big, calloused hand reaches out, takes mine, and squeezes it. For a moment, I think he looks as though he's going to cry, but that moment disappears when Odette stops.

"This D-Devon," Odette says.

I'm staring into the face of an incredibly handsome young man, maybe in his twenties. He has dark hair, and it's short and neatly cut. His big dark eyes go wide when his gaze lands on Odette's. He wears jeans with a red NBA shirt with Parker's number on it. He's his brother-in-law's number one fan, I'd guess.

Odette gestures to me. "This Dee."

I step closer and hold out my hand. He taps his leg, and his mouth clicks a few times before he extends his hand.

"It's nice to meet you, Devon," I say.

"Nice to m-meet you too."

I take his hand, then he releases it almost instantly, taps at his leg again, and clicks his mouth once more. His speech is much clearer than Odette's, but these two together are the cutest thing. He wraps his arm around Odette and places a kiss on her cheek. She grins and turns a light shade of pink.

I want to jump up and down for joy. Odette has found herself a man, and he's completely smitten with her. "You like basketball?" I ask him.

Devon nods with enthusiasm. "M-my brother p-plays. He's really g-good." More taps on his leg follow. Odette clutches his hand and beams at him while my chest swells with so much love.

I turn to Hudson, who stands beside me. "I like him."

"Yay." Odette does her happy dance again and then runs off with Devon toward the barn.

"Yeah, he's a good kid and a hard worker. Dad really likes him."

"That's great." In Odette's haste to get me to meet Devon, I didn't get a chance to take in what was going on around me. Now, I take that moment and really soak up what I'm seeing. Inside the big old barn, the stables are filled with people, including some who work with the support workers we hire for the ranch. Special needs adults and kids deserve the same treatment and should enjoy themselves. The workers are there to make sure that happens.

A kid, maybe ten, draws my attention. He's eager to get onto a pony, and the worker helping him guides him around the horse to the step. His movement is slower than a regular kid his age. He slightly wobbles, and when they come to the other side of the horse, the worker assists him onto the horse. The moment he's up in the saddle, the boy lays forward and wraps his arms around the horse's neck. The boy nuzzles his face into the pony's mane, and a huge grin spreads on his face. This place invokes those kinds of feelings.

Freedom.

Acceptance.

Care.

Love.

Everyone belongs, no matter what. That was Dad's rule from the very beginning. Kind of ironic how that didn't seem to apply to me when I wanted to be with Eli.

"Dee?" Hudson gently touches my arm, pulling me from my thoughts.

I blink and turn my focus back to him. "Sorry, spaced out for a moment."

Hud follows my gaze, and his lips turn up as he watches the boy. "Come on. Dad will be glad to see you. He'll be in his office."

A wave of uncertainty crashes into me. Is he really going to be happy to see me? I told him I hated him the last time we spoke, and then I left. No one here knows what I've gone through these past few years. Only Isla, and I swore her to secrecy the first time Eli laid a hand on me. She was and still is my sounding board.

"I'm not sure he wants to see me." I twist my fingers as I stand with Hudson by the tack room, the smell of worn leather a familiar old friend.

He moves closer and wraps his arms around me. "Trust me when I say he does. You two need to talk. That's the only way you're going to get past things."

"What about us?" I lean back and take in his pained stare.

"We're good, I hope. I know I was a jerk, and not a day went by when I didn't regret what I said. I was siding with Dad, and I hope you can f-forgive me, Dee." The crack in his voice tells me everything I need to know.

I tighten my grip around him and rest my head against his chest. "You're forgiven. But when it comes to Dad, we both know what he's like."

"A hard head," we say in unison and then laugh.

"Come on." He releases me, and I follow him through the big barn door to the back corner where Dad's office has always been. A phone ringing catches my attention. There's a desk in the corner when you step through the door — they must have moved it out here sometime over the years. I remember it being up in the main homestead. I guess Dad finally decided to keep the business separate from family — in a fashion.

It doesn't appear that anything else has really changed — it's just become a lot busier, which is always good.

We get to the familiar red door. It's shut. My chest vibrates with each heartbeat. Nerves pulse through me. *Three years.* It's been that long since we've spoken or even acknowledged each other.

Will he look the same?

Will there be the same anger in his eyes and tension between us that was there the day I walked away?

All these unknowns douse me in anxiety.

Hudson knocks on the wooden door, and with each hit, my stomach rolls. "Dad?"

"Come in." That familiar deep, gravelly voice — it's him. Dad.

Hudson grabs the handle and pushes it open, stepping through the doorway. I hang back, unsure what's going to happen. "Someone is here to see you," Hudson says.

"Who's that?" There's the clicking of a keyboard, and it's as though my feet have become lead.

Hudson sticks his head out the door and

reaches out, taking my hand and pulling me into the office. I let go of him and grip my hands together, fidgeting with my fingers.

"Hey, Dad," I say in a shaky voice.

Dad's head whips up from the computer screen. "Dee?" He sounds breathless but then his demeanor changes, and he turns back to what he was doing. "What do you want?"

A chill fills the room, and any hope I had of mending things with Dad evaporates.

Chapter 4

Delilah

"COME ON, DAD. DON'T BE like that," Hudson says, much more forcefully than I'd have thought.

"Be like what? She wants something... that's most likely the only reason she's here." Dad glares at Hudson, who gives him an equal glare in return. I guess the stare-downs still happen. Nothing new here, then. These two are as stubborn as each other.

"Do you think maybe she might have just wanted to see you? Us? Her *family*?" Hudson crosses his arms over his broad chest, his shirt fitting to his muscles perfectly.

"Don't worry about it, Hud. It's clear I'm not welcome h-here anymore." My voice cracks, but

I swallow the tears that threaten. I won't let him see that he's hurt me once again.

Hudson was wrong.

He's not happy to see me.

I knew he wouldn't be.

It's like a knife to the heart.

Dad sighs, rubbing his eyes. He turns in my direction, and I feel the weight of his stare. There's hurt there. I see it as I do in my own eyes every day in the mirror. "It's good to see you, Delilah," he says gruffly.

"Good to see you too, Dad." I hold his heavy gaze.

He drops his head to the papers littered across his desk. "You can stay in your old room. Once you're settled, you can come back down here and start answering some of these nonstop calls." With that said, he rises from behind his large oak desk and moves around it. As tall as he is, he moves swiftly in tight and uncomfortable situations. He keeps walking past Hudson and goes wide around me. I'm smacked to the past the instant I catch the scent of the Old Spice he always wears. That's never changed. I always wondered if Mom bought it in bulk just so Dad never ran out.

Since losing Mom almost ten years ago, it hasn't been easy for Dad, raising us and running the business. All of us have helped and supported each other—until I left. When I was a kid, Dad was always busy trying to keep the business afloat and hold onto the property. I've lost count of how many times Dad has had offers to buy this place, all of which he's turned down instantly in the past when I was here, but since losing touch, I wouldn't know about anything recent.

"Come on, Dee. Let's get you settled." Hudson sighs. "I'm sure the others will be happy to see you. I think they're up at the house right now. We've got more than usual coming for holidays so extra hands will be great."

"I can't wait to help out." But I'm not sure how much help I'll be when Olive arrives in a couple of days. I can't stand being away from her, but I need to prepare my family for her somehow, and after the icy reception from Dad, I'm not sure how welcoming he'll be of Olive—especially since she's Eli's daughter.

Then there's the news about Eli, but that bit of information can stay buried for a while longer.

"Sorry about Dad. He's obviously having a bad day," Hudson says.

I sense Hudson's eyes on me. I give a slight nod but say nothing, the lump in my throat clogging my voice. After a moment, he turns and heads out the door. I go to follow but stop the moment I catch a glimpse of one of the last family photographs we had taken together. It was the last one before Mom passed away.

My younger self smiles back at me. It's the smile of a girl who doesn't have a care in the world. We all have our arms around each other. Mom and Dad stare at each other. The rest of us are laughing at Odette, who's doing her familiar dance, spinning in a circle with her arms in the air. None of us could get her to stand still. I can still hear the laughter of that day. It was also the day we took the first steps to turn this place around and started helping those with similar disabilities to Odette.

Mom had such a passion and pushed to get Odette the help she needed with her therapies and medication. Her weeks were filled with doctor's appointments while Dad's were spent working on the farm. It worked for them, though. Their love story is one I've always wanted—to find a love like that. Dad has never looked at another woman the way he did Mom.

"I remember that day."

I spin toward the doorway where my younger brother, Harley, now stands in his dark blue jeans covered in what looks to be dirt.

I rush to him, throw my arms around his neck, and he wraps his around me. He squeezes so tight I choke on my words. "It's good to see you."

"I passed Hud outside, and he told me you were here. I'm so glad you're home, Dee." Harley finally releases me, and I take a big breath.

"I swear, you haven't aged a day since I left.

Can you share your secrets with me?" I laugh, taking him in. He looks so much like Dad with his dark chocolate eyes, and for some reason, he has the same stubble growing as Hudson. "What's with the unshaven look you and Hud have going?"

Harley rakes his hand through his already misplaced hairdo. "The ladies like it." He shrugs, giving me a wry grin.

I roll my eyes. "Seriously? You two need to find yourselves wives. It surely can't be that hard."

"It's mostly families who come here. It's kind of hard to meet someone, especially when the neighbors are older than you and you're on-again-off-again feuding with them, so we're told to stay away. Then there's River Valley. That's a fair drive. Who can deal with long distance?"

I shove him in the arm. "That's not long distance. It's like a two-hour drive. As for neighbors, they're not bad. You're just afraid of commitment."

"Yeah, yeah. One day, the right person will come along. You were always supposed to be the one who had the first grandchild."

My stomach drops, and I release a nervous laugh. How will he feel in a couple of days when Olive shows up?

Clearing my throat, I walk past Harley and back out into the barn. "Come on. I need to get settled and check in with the other girls."

"They're going to be happy to see you."

"Don't say that. Hudson did about Dad, and that didn't go down so well."

Harley wraps his bulky arm over my shoulder. "Don't worry about Dad. Things here have been up and down over the years. The girls going through stuff. Taking care of Odette. Taking care of the business and all that entails with the holiday stays, teaching, and therapies. It's full-on. We have plenty of help, though, which has been good. Now you're back, maybe you can bring with you some order and get some of your sisters back down here in the barn, working again. Although they are busy with their own things that help the ranch."

"Well, if they want to escape the house because I'm back, then I'm sure you'll have no problem getting them out to the barn," I joke.

"Don't let Dad's mood dampen yours. You're home, and that's more important than anything. You deserve to be here."

"Thanks for the support." My brothers usually side with Dad, so this is new territory. They sided with him the night hurtful words were slung at me like hard stones and did nothing to support me. Letting go of that anger is something I've worked hard on. I'm still not sure that I am fully there yet, either. Perhaps with this trip home, I can end that chapter of my life and move on from it all.

We're about to step out of the barn when the phone to the right rings.

"Time to sharpen those skills, sis, if you plan on staying." Harley gives me a wry grin, points to the unmanned desk and gestures to the phone. "Go ahead."

I hesitate briefly before picking it up.

Chapter 5

Sebastian

"I THINK THIS IS FOR the best. Your girls are the most important and precious people in your life. They need their dad."

I stare across the table at James, the team principal of Haze Formula One Team.

Rage.

Anger.

Frustration.

Hurt.

Loss.

A heart can only take so much.

"Will I have a spot next year, or is this it? I had plans. I was so close to world champion. I can do that again." I want to slam my hand on the table.

They're obviously not hearing me and only seeing what I've been through and using that against me.

"We know. Do you honestly think you could race now with everything going on? You need to be in a good headspace. We're grieving with you, Sebastian. We want what's best for you and your family," James says as though he's reading from a prewritten script.

"I understand, but that's why I took the last year off… to get in the right headspace. I'm ready to return to the team. Race fit," I reply with a grin, flexing my biceps as I do.

"I can't promise it's going to happen this year. I'm truly sorry, Sebastian. We had to replace you for the rest of last season, and we weren't sure where you'd be at the start of this season, so we kept Austin on along with Elliott. I promise that you'll have a spot next year. Keep in shape, and we'll have you in to do testing. I'll keep you down as a reserve driver for this year as well."

How could he do this? I understand the team and winning is more important than anything else, but how could they brush me aside like this without discussing it with me? I turn to my agent, Luke, who's wearing a look of sorrow. He tried his hardest to keep me a spot this year. Mom would've helped out with the kids, and between her, Dad, and my sisters, I could've easily managed my career.

"Whatever you say." I rise from my seat across from James and rest Ruby on my hip. "Come on, Ry. Pack up. We're heading off."

"Nana's not going to be happy," she says in a singsong tone.

My brow furrows. "What do you mean?"

"You're not racing, are you?" Her big blue eyes stare up at me. She's too observant for her own good and incredibly switched on for a five-year-old.

"Well, honey, sometimes things don't work out how we want them to. There's not much we can do about it. We can give James' number to Nana. What do you say?"

A big grin spreads across her face. "Yes, and Nana can be mad at him. She is scary when she's mad."

I chuckle. Mom probably would give James a piece of her mind, but I'm not about to upset him. I don't want to lose my chance at racing altogether.

I peek up at James. "Don't worry, James. I'm only joking."

His shoulders relax instantly. "Really, Seb. My hands are tied at the moment."

"Okay. I'll talk to you later."

After Rylee collects her stuff from the floor and puts it in her little Elsa and Anna bag, we head out, passing the familiar faces of the mechanics and technicians. They all wave a greeting, but while I grin back, my stomach churns with hurt and dismissal. They've basically thrown me to the side.

I needed to get back behind the wheel, prove to those who think I'm done that I am not, and experience that adrenaline rush of being back on the track. It's as though a part of me has been missing, and it's racing. *Anna-Beth would want me racing again.*

Luke follows silently behind me, walking beside Rylee. When we get to the car, I lock Ruby into her seat, and Rylee climbs in and pulls her seatbelt across her body. I start the car and turn to Rylee. "Daddy won't be a minute. I have to talk to Uncle Luke, okay?"

"Okay, Daddy." She picks up a chew toy for Ruby and hands it to her. Ruby's little hands grab for it, and as soon as she has it, it's in her mouth. Teething. Fun times. I take a packet of cookies from the baby bag, open it, and hand them to Rylee. "Thank you," she says and munches away.

I shut the door and turn to face Luke. "What are we going to do? Any other teams got any openings?"

Luke's blond hair swishes from side to side as he confirms what I already know. "I haven't heard anything, but I'll keep my ear to the ground and find out if something is going on."

"Luke, I need to get behind the wheel again. I

want this bad. It's a release for me. I need it to feel normal again. To be... human." I run my fingers through my hair, grip the back of my neck, and glance up to the sky before meeting his gaze once more.

"Look, take this season off. You can't expect a spot right now given their racers have been announced and the season is moving forward."

"But they should've given it back to me." My fist clenches.

"I'll do what I can. You'll race again, Seb. I've got your back, and you know how ruthless I can be." He pauses a moment, then says, "Maybe not as ruthless as Momma King, but I can do my best, or I can bring your mom with me, and she can tear into them."

We both laugh. Mom would really tear into someone if she felt they were holding me or any of my sisters back.

"I did warn you before you took me on as a client. My mother is fierce, and then comes Skylar and Ivy... those two are mini moms. I feel for their future husbands."

Luke laughs and then clears his throat. "Take some time and leave things with me. I'll figure something out. It's summer break right now, so go somewhere, enjoy some time with the girls, and then come back, and we might have something solid in place if not for now, then surely for next year."

"Yeah, yeah, okay then. Rylee has been asking me constantly if we can go on a vacation. Maybe I'll go to the place my friend mentioned to me. Rose Ridge Ranch, some homestay place. It has farm animals, lake swimming, horseback riding, and a whole heap of other things she listed off, but I can't think of them right now."

Luke nods his approval. "Sounds like the perfect holiday destination. I think it's what you and the girls need."

I sigh. "You're right. Their happiness is something I can control right now, and I need to give them time before I get back to work. Thanks for the push." I hold out my hand, and he takes it. We shake, and then I pull him into a one-armed hug and release him. "Thanks for having my back."

"I've always got it. Now, go spend some downtime with your girls and let me do the work."

We part ways, and I climb into the car. Pulling my phone from my pocket, I shoot a text to Simone.

> **Sebastian:** *Looks like I'm finally heading to the place you suggested for a getaway. Rose Ridge, wasn't it?*

Her response is instant.

> **Simone:** *Yeah, it is. We just got back from there. Some friends, April and Spencer Cook, were there recently. They loved it. It's such a peaceful place. It recharges my mental batteries. How are things going? How are the girls? I can't wait to see them again.*

Sebastian: Things are going okay. I haven't been able to get a seat to race, which is driving me nuts. Luke is handling that, though. The girls are doing good—getting bigger, and Ry is just so smart and is becoming more and more like her mother. Ruby is chubby, cute, and a teething monster. All in all, we're doing good, but I'm being forced on vacation so I'm going to take time out from the world and all the opinions on my racing and how I'm raising my family.

Simone: You're doing the best you can. You got dealt a bad hand, and my heart hurts for you and the girls, but I know how strong you are. And you're such a great dad. I'm here if you need anything. You know that.

Sebastian: I know, and I really appreciate it. I'm going to book now for Rose Ridge.

Simone: Mention me, and you'll get a discount. They know me pretty well.

Sebastian: Okay, will do. Thanks. I'll check in later.

Simone: Take care.

I google the ranch and then search for a contact number. I hit dial, and it rings a few times before a female voice answers, "Rose Ridge Ranch, you're speaking with Delilah."

"Hey, Delilah, I'm wanting to book a stay in one of your cabins for myself and my daughters, please."

"Ah, okay, yep." She sounds flustered, and I can hear the click of keys on a computer, and she curses under her breath as I hear something drop. Not a good start to the week for her, maybe.

"Is everything okay?" I ask.

"Yeah, sorry. It's been a while since I've done this. Give me a moment, and I'll get someone who actually knows what the heck they're doing. Sorry, I'm a little all over the place. I'm not usually the one who answers the phone, as you can probably tell. I'm not so great at this job." She laughs nervously.

I chuckle. "It's all right. Take your time. I'm not in a rush." I turn in my seat and check the girls, and they're happy playing. That won't last much longer for Ruby, as her coos slowly start turning into little cries. She hates her car seat when the car isn't moving.

After a few more curse words and some muttering, Delilah comes back on the phone. "Sorry about that. First time on the phones in a couple of years. What dates are you after?"

"Um... I was hoping for tomorrow, and I currently don't have an end date. It's for me and my two daughters. Do you cater for almost one and five-year-olds?"

"Of course, it's all ages around here. Plenty for everyone to do and enjoy." I hear the smile in her voice. "We have some cabins available. So arriving tomorrow, and I'll add a tentative departure date for the system, perhaps just a couple of weeks, and we can adjust as we need to."

"I'd like that very much."

"What's your name, sir?" she asks, not sounding so flustered anymore.

"Sebastian King."

Silence.

"Hello?" I ask, checking to make sure she's still on the line, but the call is still connected.

And I have no idea why she's gone so quiet, but I hope it doesn't mean she's heard all the stories about my racing and parenting too.

Chapter 6

Delilah

THIS MUST BE MY BROTHERS playing some kind of joke on me. I turn to Harley, who's standing nearby, tapping on the computer to bring up the bookings page. It's a system I haven't used before but looks straightforward.

I cock an eyebrow. His eyes go wide, and he shrugs, mouthing, *"What?"*

"*The* Sebastian King?" I ask, slightly breathless, and as I speak his name, Harley's mouth drops, and he scrambles to change the cabin he's picked to one of our top ones.

"The one and only." His voice is deep and sexy. I mean, he's a hot Formula One driver. One of my favorites.

"Wow!" I breathe. "For a moment, I thought

my brothers were playing a welcome-home prank on me."

Sebastian laughs on the other end, and my stomach swirls with excitement. *The* Sebastian King is coming here. "This isn't a prank."

"Well, I'm glad to hear that. So, we have you booked in?" I ask.

He's silent for a moment, but I can hear a small child in the background—oh, his sweet girls. I was so sad to hear about the loss of his wife. She was always trackside supporting him whenever she could. Their love was never hidden. She was the first person he went to after winning a race, kissing her and their daughter, and then jumping on his team and celebrating.

"I guess we'll see you tomorrow."

My breath seizes in my lungs for a split second. "I look forward to it." Harley puts that last bit of information and payment details in the computer and then stands, placing his hands on his head.

"Thank you. My friend, Simone, has been on me to stay there. She was just there, and her friends still are."

"Wow, I'm glad Simone recommended us," I say.

Harley nods furiously, scribbles down something on a pad near the phone, and holds it up for me to read.

Simone is friends with Spencer
Cook's wife. They're staying
here right now.

My mouth drops open for the second time in the space of ten minutes. Spencer Cook, the famous quarterback, is staying here too?

Sebastian King's voice pulls me out of my fan craze. "I've been meaning to come for a while, but things have been crazy."

Yeah, I'm sure they have, is what I want to say, but it's not my place. "I'm sorry to hear that. We'll have your cabin set up for you to arrive tomorrow." Keep it together, Delilah. Keep it together. My heartbeats are going crazy. Here I am talking to one of the best drivers in Formula One. I missed seeing him on the track last season.

"That's great. Thanks so much."

"Thanks again, Sebastian."

"Thanks, Delilah. See you then," he says.

I hang up the phone and release a breath while clutching my chest. Leaning over, I take several deep breaths.

"Please tell me that was who I think it was because obviously, I've already given him one of the best cabins we have. I mean, they're all good, but this one has great views of the hills and is privately secluded given who he is. He's near Spencer Cook's cabin. I wonder if they know each other?" Harley keeps talking like he's had a shot of straight caffeine.

I finally manage to settle my heart rate back down to normal. Turning, I rest my hands on his shoulders, shaking him. "It was him. I can't believe it. I honestly thought you and Hudson were playing a joke on me."

"What about me?"

Harley and I spin toward Hudson, who has just entered the barn, and stares at us in confusion.

Hudson cocks his eyebrow. "It's always you two up to no good, isn't it? What have you done now?"

I smack his arm. "Guess who we have coming here?" I breathe excitedly, unable to control the thrill coursing through me.

Hudson's gaze shifts from me to Harley and then back to me. "Well, who?"

"Sebastian King," I whisper to refrain from screaming it and scaring all the people and animals.

Hudson crosses his arms and purses his lips into a thin line. "Nice try, you two."

"No, Hud, we're not kidding," Harley says before spinning the computer screen in his direction.

Hudson leans in and reads the booking page. Slowly, his face morphs into something else. Those hazel eyes go wide, and his eyebrows shoot to the sky. "Oh... so you're not kidding?"

Harley and I glance at each other, grinning stupidly. I do a little dance on my toes, the excitement uncontrollable.

I turn back. "Not kidding, and is it true you have Spencer Cook, the quarterback, staying here?"

Both men chuckle. "It's been a while, sis, and we've gathered a good clientele of famous people who like to come here to get away from the press and escape the hassles of the world and media scrutiny. We do try to maintain a level of formality if you get what I'm saying. No fangirl moments." Hudson's gaze narrows in on me.

I huff. "Yeah, I get it. I can be cool, calm, and collected. I hope…" I throw a sideways glance to Hudson, who shakes his head, folding his arms across his broad chest.

"Come on, I'm sure the girls would like to see you. Mabel is in town getting supplies, so we can surprise her when she gets back."

My stomach drops. I left Olive in town. I thought for sure they wouldn't be in town. I hope Isla hasn't gone out.

"Hey, Dee, are you all right?" Harley gently grabs my arm.

Nodding, I attempt to shake the fear away. "Yeah, sorry. Just switched off for a split second. Mabel is in town, got it. Where are Talulla and Sybil?"

Hudson answers as he pats a horse that's being

led past us. "They're up at the house. Talulla has a therapy session shortly, and Sybil is probably rebelling somewhere. Do you remember your hate-the-world-and-everything-in-it stage?"

How could I forget? "Oh, to be twenty again and put you all through hell," I joke.

"I think you've already done enough of that," Dad's familiar yet monotone voice says from behind me. A stab of hurt runs through my heart like a red-hot poker. My face heats and tears sting my eyes. Turning around, I face my father.

"It's good to know you're still being a jerk," I berate him. My body trembles and I want so badly to yell at him, but I won't do it here. I was hoping to avoid this kind of confrontation, but his words sting, so I lash out. "And you wonder why I stayed away so long, Dad. You... this?" I wave my hand between us as my voice shakes. "I had hoped you would be past it all, but I guess not. I was planning on staying, but now I'm not so sure I want to. Not with this icy welcome from you."

I turn and stride out the barn door before he even gets the chance to reply. I didn't come here to relive that damaging time of my life. I'm already carrying a weight on my shoulders they all know nothing about.

Chapter 7

Delilah

THE DIRT CRUNCHES UNDER MY shoes as I walk away from the barn and Dad with his hurtful words. I head back toward the main homestead—the family home. It's an expansive stone and brick building with a large patio with white beams and a fern hanging off every wooden post. It still looks good. I have so many memories within those walls—good and bad. The good outweighs the bad, but still, the hurt is simmering. It will boil over if Dad keeps pressing my buttons.

I stop in front of the house and stare at the closed screen door. Familiar voices filter out—probably Sybil and Odette since Mabel isn't here. Perhaps I should leave. It's clear Dad isn't keen to even try to fix things. I might be stirring up too many ghosts and hurtful things from the past that should stay buried. I need my family, though, even if Dad isn't on board yet. Time is what's needed to heal old wounds.

I take a step back, and large hands catch my arms.

"You do realize you can go in? It's your home," Harley says gently and gives me a soft nudge toward the door.

"I'm not so sure anymore. Dad doesn't want me here, and for all I know, neither does anyone else."

Harley comes around and stands in front of me. His eyes bore into mine. A hint of anger and hurt radiate from them. He grips my arms again. "Don't think like that. Hudson and I know we were major douches when everything blew up. We sided with Dad without even thinking about you and what you might have been going through. We're genuinely happy to see you."

His words mean so much to my fragile heart. I needed to hear them spoken by family. If he knew the dark place I've been these past six months, he'd know they hold so much power for me in this moment.

Olive is my main reason for living. If I didn't have her, I'd have had nothing worth fighting for on my deathbed almost a year ago. "Harley…"

"No, no more. This is your home, and you're

welcome back here any time. You need to be here, sis. I can see it in your eyes. The last few years haven't been kind to you. No one else will probably see it, but I do. I learned to read you a long time ago. You were happy with Eli, and I saw it. When you're ready, I'm all ears. No judgment." He pulls me into his arms, and we stand there for a moment. Harley's hugs are always the best—like he's draping a big security blanket over me. He's safety.

The familiar squeak of the screen door tears us apart.

Talulla comes to a halt in the doorway. "So, you're back? I thought Odette was playing a joke on me." Her hands go to her hips, and she stares daggers at Harley and me.

"I not joking," Odette says adamantly with a stomp of her foot from behind Talulla, who moves out of her way.

Talulla turns to her. "I know that, Odette. It's okay." The softness of her words to Odette only confirms she's mad at me. Now, her icy blue gaze is back on me. She's the younger version of me. We're the only two in the family with blonde hair, blue eyes, and olive complexions—we're Mom's lookalikes. How will Tally take to Olive?

"Why didn't you tell us you were coming? How long are you staying?" Talulla finally asks. I can't tell if she's happy to see me or not, but her body language and tone tell me no.

"Tally, let's go inside and get some lunch. I'm sure Dee will fill you in and answer all your questions," Harley suggests, trying to simmer the situation.

She turns, her blonde ponytail whipping around behind her and then swaying from side to side as she pulls the screen door open and disappears through the doorway.

"Well, I guess she's mad at me as well." I sigh and rub my hand down my face. I've only been here a short while, but I'm exhausted. Stirring up all these emotions and memories has worn me out.

"Don't worry. I'm sure she'll come around easy enough. This is Little Miss Saint we're talking about."

I laugh. "Yes, very true." Tally has a way of not staying mad for long. When we were growing up, Harley broke one of her Barbie dolls, and she was mad for about thirty minutes then forgave him.

Stepping through the doorway is like going back in time. Everything is the same as it was the day I packed my bags and left. It's as if I'm walking down memory lane. The walls are painted crisp white with dark blue trimming on the doorframes. Family pictures line the hall. The smell of cookies baking twists my heart. It reminds me of Mom.

"Tally bakes?" I turn to Harley, unable to hide my surprise.

"Yep. She's as good as Mom, if not better. We've got a kitchen down in one of the smaller sheds, and she leads classes with our holiday-stay guests and one-on-one sessions with clients. Simple cooking skills for those special needs people who need it. It's amazing how much they all learn here. They're smarter than the world gives them credit for."

"Oh, I completely understand that. What Dad did with this place is nothing short of amazing. These people's lives are changed, and they're taught skills no other place currently offers."

"Quit taking your time and get in here," Tally yells from the kitchen. Harley and I grin at each other and make our way down the hall and into an open dining and kitchen area.

This part of the house has changed—it's become more modern. There are white cupboards and black marble countertops with stainless-steel appliances. It's huge. If I loved baking or cooking, I'd stay in here all day and never leave. It's never been my strong suit— horses have.

My gaze lands on a range of different-colored iced cookies sitting on the countertop. "These look great, Tally." I move to the opposite side of the counter and take a seat so I don't get in her way.

"Thanks. You can have one. It's Mom's recipe."

Without hesitation, Harley and I snatch one, and we both take a bite. The sugar cookie melts in my mouth. Harley was right—in fact, these are better than Mom's, but the memories of the cookies all belong to her, especially at Christmas time. These were Mom's specialties.

"These are amazing," I say between bites.

Tally shrugs. "I know. I've mastered it. Dad wouldn't let me help out much with the therapies since I'm not fully qualified, and you know me. Sometimes horses scare me because they're such big animals." Her body shakes as she says the words. "So, I took to the kitchen and did an online course, and now I have a qualification in cooking and can teach the kids and any others who need it."

I beam at her, a proud sister. "That's really great, Tally. You're doing something amazing for these people. They need someone like you teaching them those skills. I might need to get you in the saddle, though."

"I'm not so sure. They scare me. Give me a motorbike any day." She laughs nervously, and it's almost like I never left. We'd have these kinds of conversations around the dining table. I loved those times and miss them. I want Olive to have these experiences, and she will as she grows up.

"You took to the motorbikes pretty quickly," I say.

"That's because she wouldn't get on the dang

horse," Harley jokes as he stands in front of the refrigerator. Tally kicks out and hits him in the butt with her foot.

"Shut up. I'm not the horse whisperer like this one here," she says, jerking a thumb in my direction.

"That's a name I haven't heard in a while. I've probably lost my mojo, it's been so long." While Tally's back is turned, I snatch another cookie. They're addictive. I know what my midnight snack is going to be tonight.

"You can work your magic tomorrow. I'm heading to the horse sale yards in the morning. You wanna come?" Harley asks as he takes some food from the refrigerator and then piles meat and condiments onto some bread.

Going to the yards was something I used to do with Dad. "Is Dad coming?"

He shakes his head. "No, he hasn't been since you left, now that I think about it." His brow furrows, then he shrugs and goes back to his sandwich.

"Oh, okay. Yeah, I'll come then. What time?"

"The usual... early. Have to get in there first thing in the morning to get the good ones, or at least the ones you think are good. No one has come close to you in picking the good horses. You should go down and see your horse, Holly. I bet she'd remember you. After all, you saved her."

I finish the last bit of my cookie and say,

"Wow, it's been so long. She'd probably bite me for leaving her."

"Maybe. She still bites Hudson and me but won't bite girls, so Mabel takes care of her," Harley says with a full mouth of food.

The day we brought Holly home, she was skin and bones. She'd been left in a stall most of her life. I wanted to hit the man who was selling her—he wanted top dollar for her. When Dad saw how Holly reacted to me, he didn't hesitate. I can read the animals—obviously better than I read people.

"Okay, well, I'm happy to go. Is there anything I can do to help around here for the rest of the day?" I ask, glancing between Tally and Harley.

"I'm not sure. Why not get your stuff settled in your room and then go down and see Holly. Just have a day gathering yourself? Tomorrow, you'll go horse shopping with Harley. After that, I'm sure you'll be busy," Tally suggests as she takes a fresh tray of cookies from the oven and places them one by one on a cooling rack.

"Sure, that sounds good." Silence fills the room briefly before Harley takes the remainder of his sandwich, bids us farewell, and heads back out the front door.

"Your room is… well, you already know where it is." Tally shrugs and grabs the bowl of premixed cookie dough and flour from another counter, the room suddenly turning icy.

Rising from my seat, I ask, "Is there something you want to say? Just get it off your chest. I'm already dealing with Dad and his snide remarks, so just lay it on me."

Tally stops flouring the counter. Her eyes lock with mine. "I'm allowed to be annoyed with you. Not once did you contact me. You contacted Sybil but not me. Not Mabel, either, and I'm surprised the boys even welcomed you back like they did." She huffs out a breath and shuffles on her feet before dropping her gaze back to what she was doing.

"I get it. I'm the one who walked away. There was nothing stopping anyone from reaching out to me, either." I keep my words even and calm. Anger isn't the answer here. I'm sure Mabel is going to have her say as well. They have every right to feel how they want.

She throws the dough onto the floured counter, and it blows up and covers her black flour-covered apron. "That's not the point, Dee. You left. *You left.* You went with *him,* and where the hell is he now, huh? You've come crawling back. Why? What do you want?" As she speaks each of her words it's like I'm being whipped over and over. The sting ripples through my body.

I bite my lip to refrain from losing my composure. My eyes burn with unshed tears. If only she knew the truth. I could tell her, but I'm not ready to talk about Eli with her in this state. I'm not throwing that at her and then having her feel bad about slandering him.

Tally continues, "Why did you come home, Dee? What's so important that you *have* to be here?" Her words tremble, and instead of answering her questions, I step around and come to stand in front of her, pulling her into my arms.

A tear slides down my face. I hate my family seeing me weak. Reaching up, I swipe it away and let the mixture of love, hurt, and anger swirl around us like a tornado. I say the only thing I can at this moment. "I'm sorry."

Chapter 8

Delilah

TALLY DIDN'T ACKNOWLEDGE MY APOLOGY, but it's a start, so I leave her to her baking. It's clear I have some fences to mend with my siblings—that's a lot of work to do. I should've done better. It was Dad I had the problem with, and I held the words he slung at me against all of them.

After grabbing my bags from the car, I make my way back through the front door and head upstairs. Pictures of myself and my siblings line the walls—me with my ribbons at the horse shows, the boys in their bull-riding outfits and holding their trophies, Tally dressed up as a cowgirl for Halloween with Sybil as a little witch and Odette a ghost. I chuckle to myself because Odette has her hands in the air, spinning once again. This wall was Mom's pride and joy. She was always updating the pictures or shuffling them around.

Slowly, I make my way down the hallway. I pass all the rooms and stop at the study's closed door — Mom's little library. I'm suddenly whipped back to a time when we'd sit in there. We'd read and have lots of chats and laughs together.

I drop my bags. My hand hovers over the handle. I grip it and turn, and the door welcomes me back with its familiar creak as I push it open. A dusty, musty smell hits my nose and causes me to cough.

I'm met with darkness.

The curtains are closed.

Reaching in, my hand hits the wall until I find the light switch and flick it on.

A tidal wave of sadness washes over me as I take in the room. White sheets cover all the furniture and the bookshelves that line the walls.

Why is it like this?

The window seat where Mom and I used to sit is also covered. The floors are the only thing not shrouded in white. I walk over. Dust lines the window ledge. It's like they've covered over the memories I hold most dear. I can't deal with this right now. I race back out the way I came, clicking the light off and shutting the door behind me. I take one deep breath after another to calm my erratic heart.

"When you left, Dad shut the door and never went back in there."

I whirl around toward Hudson's gentle voice. "Why?" I sob. *Oh goodness, when did I start crying?*

His broad shoulders shrug. "No one knows for sure. My guess is that it was Mom's room first, and he lost her, then it became your room, and he lost you too. Perhaps he didn't want to risk losing another person he loves."

My chest tightens. "Oh, Hud…" My legs crumble beneath me. Hudson quickly gets to me before I'm on the floor. "I messed up everything."

He pulls me tightly against him, holding me upright. "No, you didn't."

"Yes, I did. Everyone is mad at me, but no one understands anything that I've been through."

"That's because you haven't told us. We haven't spoken."

"And I don't want to. Not right now. It's still too raw." I cry into his shirt, gripping him tightly. I need to put a lid on my emotions. Letting it out all at once isn't a good idea. It's too painful.

"I get it, Dee. I get it."

"You think you get it, but none of you do. I'm fine with handling all the anger and hurt everyone has against me. I've dealt with much worse over the past three years." I tear myself away from him and pick up my bags, turning my back to him and heading to yet another room that might maim me with memories.

Hudson doesn't come after me. *Good.* I don't want to talk anymore.

Opening the door, I keep the light off and go straight to the bed. I don't care if it's got dust all over it like Mom's library. I collapse on top of the covers. My eyes close, and I'm swept into a nightmare.

A gentle knock on my door startles me awake. "Dee?" Sybil's voice filters through from the other side.

"Yeah?" I respond, still trying to wake up. I glance out the window, and what little sun was shining through the crack in the curtains is gone. I've slept all afternoon. What time is it?

"Can I come in?"

"Sure."

The door clicks open. "Well, now I know why you've slept all afternoon. It's pitch black in here. No wonder you're sleeping the day away." She flicks the light on.

I throw my arm over my eyes, the brightness too much for my sleepy state. "I just wanted to sleep."

"I guessed that, so I let you. I came to find you before, but Hudson said you'd come in here and hadn't seen you again. He mentioned you were pretty upset."

The bed dips, and I shuffle over to give her some room. Rubbing my eyes, I sit up, and I'm finally able to take in my old room. Running my fingers over the bed covers, there's no dust. It's all clean. The dresser is spotless, with photographs in place that I'd left behind. The floor is now tidy. When I left, I was in a hurry and just packed what I could at the time, throwing discarded items on the floor. Dark blue curtains hang over the window. It's exactly how I remember it.

As if reading my thoughts, Sybil says, "I'd wash the sheets and clean in here often in the hopes that you'd come home one day. And look at that… you're here." She smiles, her chocolate eyes crinkling at the corners and that single dimple in her cheek.

"Thanks for that. After seeing the library, I wasn't sure what to expect in here."

"Dad won't let any of us go in there. I've snuck in a couple of times to try to clean up, but it's as though he has a sixth sense about someone being in that room, and the moment I start dusting, he's in the doorway. His glare is enough for me to hightail it out of there. Dad's just a grumpy old man now," she jokes, and it brings a smile to my face.

"I'll clean it up after I settle in." Speaking of settling in, I need to ring Isla and see how Olive is going.

"I wanted to come say hey and to let you know that dinner is ready. Mabel is home now as well. She wants to see you, so I told her I'd check if you were awake."

I yawn and ask, "Is she mad at me as well?"

"I don't know. If she is, she didn't show it." Sybil gets up and says, "Get ready and come down for dinner."

I nod, and she leaves. A family dinner is waiting downstairs for me. Will Dad be there? Is it going to end with someone in tears?

After sorting myself and getting somewhat freshened up, I make my way down. Voices filter through the house, and when I begin my descent down the stairs, I pause. They're discussing me.

"Sybil, you kept in contact with her?" There's an accusation in Mabel's words.

"Yeah, I did. None of you did, did you?" She sounds angry and accusing.

"Sybil, did she tell you anything about what was going on?" Hudson asks. I stay stock-still, not wanting the stairs to creak as I move. They were always an alarm of some kind when I was growing up.

"She told me everything was going good," Sybil replies.

"She's not good. From what I saw this afternoon, she's far from it, Syb. I've never witnessed her in that kind of state," Hudson says.

"I don't know what to tell you guys. Perhaps she's been keeping things from me. We have to be there for her," Sybil says.

"Yeah, right. She hasn't been there for me, so

why should I be there for her?" Tally's still angry. My face flushes with heat. I should've been there for them. It's partly my fault, the rift between myself and my siblings.

"Tally, you can't be like that. There's a lot of hurt within these walls, not only for us but for her as well. And with Dad being a jerk, she's going to have a hard time getting through to him," Sybil says softly. Her words cause a lump to form in my throat.

"I don't care. She abandoned us. Why should we care about what she's going through?" Tally asks. I guess my apology didn't work, but I won't stop trying with her.

"Get over yourself, Tally," Sybil snaps, and I've heard enough.

I make enough noise as I walk downstairs to alert them to my presence. I enter the open dining and kitchen area. All eyes are on me, each set a weight holding me in place. My siblings and I are under the same roof once again.

"Dee, I'm so glad you're home." Mabel rushes to me from where she stood near the table and wraps me in her arms. She may be tiny, but she sure can squeeze tight when hugging. She has beauty like an open rose but the bite of a thorn on a bush.

"Good to see you too," I manage to say as she nearly cuts off my airway. Mabel realizes and releases me.

"Come on. Let's have some food," she says and gestures to the pre-set table. A feast is laid out—salads, cooked beef, and something that looks like marinated chicken.

"Wow, thank you to whoever prepared this." I take in everyone in the room, and their eyes drift to Tally. "Thanks, Tally."

She waves her hand and goes to the refrigerator, then comes to the table with some drinks. I take my seat and notice Dad's seat is empty. "Where's Dad?"

"I've taken some food to him down in his office. He said he had some paperwork to finish off," Sybil says and takes a serving spoon for the potato salad, but when I look around the table, no one meets my gaze.

Clearly, he's avoiding me.

"Oh, okay."

No one says another word.

We all dig into the salads and eat mostly in silence, apart from the odd question here or there. No one asks about Eli or what I've been doing. Good. I don't want to answer those questions yet, and when Olive gets here, I'm sure they'll ask those and plenty more.

Once we finish, we all sit around the large table. Harley and Hudson chat about the horse sales tomorrow, and Tally clears the table with Mabel helping her. Odette is engrossed in her iPad. Devon comes in a little late but takes a seat next to Odette. They're so cute. It's as though they understand each other and respect one another. It's beautiful. I'm so glad she's been able to find someone who makes her happy.

"Dee is coming with me tomorrow to the yards," Harley announces.

Hudson's head turns in my direction, and he cocks his eyebrow. "The horse whisperer, you mean. I'm interested in seeing what she comes back with. They're usually the ones that need the most work."

"Yeah, are you going to be around long enough to help with that, Dee?" Tally sneers as she loudly places plates in the sink.

"Enough, Tally." Sybil sighs.

"It's okay, she's entitled to her remarks. I'm not dignifying you with a response. I've apologized to you. Do with it what you want. Continue to hate me, I don't care. I'm going to my room." As I rise from my chair, it scrapes on the floor. I turn to Harley. "I'll see you in the morning."

"The usual time," he says.

I nod and escape the room knowing full well they'll be having a heated conversation once I leave. I hope Odette and Devon aren't there for that. They don't need their happy spirits squashed. When I get to the bottom of the stairs leading back to my room, Odette's voice booms.

"Why you so mean, Tally?" She genuinely sounds hurt.

I don't hear anything else as I escape upstairs, taking two steps at a time.

This family will need some time to mend, and it's all because I fell in love with the farmhand, and Dad didn't approve. There's no stopping love, even when that love hurts so much, it leaves bruises, and that's what Eli did. He left many colors on my skin in various places.

I couldn't leave, though.

I loved him as much as I did when I'd first left with him.

No one would or could understand.

Things are different now — I'm different. I see Eli for what he really was and still is — the monster who haunts my dreams.

Chapter 9

Sebastian

"MAKE SURE YOU TAKE A small first-aid kit and lots of warm clothes." Mom gives me my list of what to pack for the girls while we're away.

"I know, Mom. I know how to pack for my kids." I sigh. She does this all the time. I should be used to it, but with Mom, no matter how many times I tell her I know, it's never enough. She'll continue to be the overbearing grandmother. It's good for them to have a strong female figure in their life to look up to. I couldn't ask for a better role model, though. Sandra King is Momma King to many of the closest people in my life. She'd take my friends in and feed them like they were strays living on the street.

"Honey, you haven't gone away for any length

of time with them. Perhaps I should come with you."

"Thanks for the offer, but I've got it." I remove the phone from my ear and put it on speaker, placing it on the bed so I can get these last few things packed.

"You might need some help with them," she pushes.

"Mom, I love you, but let me learn on my own. It's been almost a year. I'm sure I can manage. I *have* been managing just fine."

"Are you running away because it's the first anniversary of Anna-Beth's death?"

Loss slams into me once again. Her name is a punch to the stomach, winding me.

"I've got to go, Mom. I'll talk to you later." I throw a shirt in the suitcase and pause, rubbing my forehead.

She doesn't argue but says goodbye, and we hang up.

"Was that Gram?" Rylee comes in and jumps up on the bed, causing the phone to bounce around.

I pick up a pair of socks and place them in a suitcase. "It was. She wanted to come on our holiday with us."

"Really? That would be fun."

I stop and glance up at her. She looks like a mini of her mother. Her black hair is tied up in two little pigtails. That's one hairstyle I've mastered. We're still dealing with her not liking me brushing her hair, so there are plenty of tears by the time those pigtails are tied up. Anna-Beth was so good at it. I never heard Rylee cry when she did it. Perhaps it's my beefy hands that pull too tight. Whatever it is, she screams as though I'm physically hurting her whenever I take a brush to her hair.

"This is our little vacation. Don't you want to spend some time with Dad?" I ask, reaching out, tickling her, that familiar high-pitched giggle filling the room.

"I always spend time with you, Daddy. Gram is fun too." She hands me a shirt that had fallen off the bed.

"She's lots of fun. How about if we go for a little while on our own, and then *maybe* we can get Gram to come down?"

Her eyes go wide, and her grin turns huge. "Yes, that would be lots of fun."

She wanders out of my room, but I know she'll be back. Thankfully, Ruby is taking her nap, so I can get these things done. Teething babies aren't much fun. Anna-Beth dealt with that kind of stuff with Ry. It's opened my eyes to many things I missed with Ry—even the crappy times. Anna-Beth would ring Mom if I was away and needed help. Mom really is an amazing person.

Moving on to the last bag to pack—mine—I

stride into my walk-in closet and take some shirts from my drawers. I pause and stare at the racks that still have some coats and shirts hanging there that belonged to Anna-Beth. Reaching out, I grip the sleeve of a bright pink coat, it was one of her favorites. She wore it at the track more times than I can count. Perhaps she wore it so I would always see her first at the end of a race. Guilt washes over me like ice-cold water, startling me from the memory. A lump forms in my throat, I swallow it down and go back to my duffle bag, shoving my shirts inside.

"Hey, Dad. It's almost Ruby's birthday, isn't it?" Ry comes bouncing back in and climbs back up onto my king-size bed. It's pretty lonely now and has been for the last almost year, another reminder of not just my loss, but *our* loss—mine and the girls.

"It is."

"Does that mean it's been one year since the accident?"

I pause. I'm not ready for this conversation. Clearing my throat, I say, "Um… yeah, baby. It's almost one year." I choke on my words which come out almost like a whisper.

She's silent for a beat. "Do you think Mommy is watching over me?" Rylee's head drops as she stares at her fingers in her lap, playing with the bottom of her little pink skirt. I pause and take in her little princess features. Tears fill her eyes as she continues to finger the hem of her clothing. My chest hurts and the ache never really subsides each time Anna-Beth is brought up. What always comes back to me is the memory of our fight I never got to fix.

I come around the other side of the bed and take a seat on the edge. I grab Ry and place her on my lap, wrapping my arms around her and squeezing tightly. "I have no doubt Mommy is watching over you and your sister."

"What about you?"

I smile, but inside, it's turmoil. The pain I thought I'd dealt with is working its way right to the surface. I attempt to swallow that all-too-familiar lump of emotions that catches in my throat. "I'm sure she's looking out for me too. I think she's been guiding me when it comes to Ruby. I need all the help I can get." I laugh, giving Rylee another tight hug, mostly for me, though. I wish Anna-Beth was here with us.

"You're a good dad, Daddy. I love you," she whispers into my chest.

"I love you too. Is there something special we should do for Ruby's birthday?" I ask. *And Mom's death.* It's forever going to be a battle of emotions when it comes to Ruby's birthday. Hopefully, it'll become a little easier as the years go by. I'd hate for Ruby to grow up and think the worst on her special day. It's a day for living and one for remembering at the same time.

"Cake?" Ry's high-pitched voice practically screams. This girl has a cake addiction.

I chuckle. "Yes, we can get a cake. What kind should we get?" Glancing up from the little girl in my lap, I take in my bedroom. It's almost all still the same. I've packed up most of Anna-Beth's things. Anna-Beth's bedside table still has one of the necklaces on it I'd given her—it has an R on it for Rylee. Her toiletries sit under the sink in the bathroom in a toiletries bag. I can't bring myself to throw absolutely everything out. This kind of thing takes time, the therapist had said.

Rylee's voice pulls me away from those hard memories. "Vanilla, with pink icing and sprinkles."

"I think we can manage that. She'll love it."

"Can we do one for Mommy but with purple icing?"

Tears fill my eyes. "I think she'd really like that." I bring Rylee up and hug her. As my tears fall, her little arms hold me tightly.

"It's okay, Daddy," she whispers in my ear and then pulls back. She reaches up and wipes away my tears. This girl is a replica of her mother, who would do that to me if something was going on and I was having a hard time. Emotions run high when I'm racing.

"It will be okay. Thanks, beautiful. Should we finish packing before Ruby wakes up, and then we can head off?" I ask.

"Yes. I can't wait. Is there going to be horses?"

"From what I've seen on their website, I believe so."

"Can I learn to ride a horse?" The excitement in her voice brings a wide grin to my face. Rylee is all the therapy I need at this time. Her heart is so big, and I know Anna-Beth would be so proud of her and how she has handled everything this past year.

My stomach twists as a small bout of anxiety creeps in. These are things I'm going to let her do. Anna-Beth and I agreed a long time ago that we wouldn't stop our kids from trying new things by instilling fear in them. They have every right to dream big just like we did.

"We'll find you the best teacher who'll help you. How does that sound?"

"Thanks, Daddy." She wriggles off my lap and takes off out the door. I lean over and drop my face into my hands, my elbows digging into my knees. This is hard. Here I thought racing was a challenge—it's nothing compared to caring for a newborn and a five-year-old tween. Give me a race car any day.

"Oh, Anna-Beth, I wish you were here and taking this holiday with us." It's become a thing lately where I sometimes talk to her, especially in moments like these when I wish so much that she was here. I'm not sure I'll ever be able to move on. How does someone recover from such a big loss? "We miss you. I miss you."

Chapter 10

Delilah

My ALARM GOES OFF, BUT I've been lying in bed awake for the past hour, in the darkness, listening to the creatures of the night. After storming off to my room last night, I rang Isla, gave her the lowdown on what happened, and told her to keep Olive there for an extra day while things hopefully settle down a bit more. When the house was quiet, I went down and grabbed a handful of cookies and sat up chatting with Isla for a while. She deserved an earful for lying to me, but I'm also glad she did.

Her question replays in my mind. *"Why not tell them about Eli and everything that happened?"*

I can't tell them—not yet.

I don't want them to be nice to me because they feel sorry for me. I don't want their sympathy. I want them to accept me, accept Olive, and when the time is right, I'll tell them what happened. I have the weight of the world resting on my shoulders, and it's slowly becoming too much.

After sitting up, I move to the side of my double bed. My feet touch the soft carpet. I rub the sleep from my eyes and then get up to flick the light on. Getting out of bed in the morning isn't an issue for me anymore since having Olive. She kept me up most of the time through the night when she was younger. Thankfully, she's getting better and it won't last forever.

Going to my suitcase on the floor, I pull out a pair of dark blue skinny-leg jeans, a black top, and a long-sleeve button-up shirt like the one I used to wear around the ranch. It may be a little cool first thing in the morning, but as the day progresses and we work in the sun, it heats up pretty quickly. I imagine that I'll be busy after the morning with the horses if we manage to get any.

Going to another of my many bags, I take out my boots. They're well worn, even to the point where the shoe's main body and sole are separated in some places. I couldn't throw them out, though—these are the shoes Mom bought me before she passed away. Thankfully, my feet are the one thing that hasn't changed size in the last three years. I slip them on, tie the laces, and make my way to the kitchen where a light is shining. Harley must already be waiting for me.

Entering the kitchen, I stop. Dad sits at the table, sipping on a steaming cup of coffee. He glances up and just stares.

I blink and then say, "Morning." I try not to come across as too happy, but I'm glad he's down here.

He mumbles, "Morning." There's silence once again before he says, "There's coffee." Then he goes back to whatever it is he's looking at on his laptop open in front of him.

"Thanks." I busy myself making my strong black coffee with some sugar.

"Will Eli be gracing us with his presence?" Dad's question isn't malicious—it sounds as though he's genuinely interested.

My mug freezes before my mouth, a lump forming in my throat. "Um… no. He…"

Before I can finish my sentence, Harley steps into the kitchen. "Hey, Dee. Morning, Dad. Any of that left?" He nods at my mug.

"Uh, yeah."

"You might want to put it in a travel mug because we're about to leave." Harley opens a cupboard and produces two reusable travel mugs, placing one on the counter near me.

I take a small sip and then tip the rest into the cup. "Dad, is there a chance for us to talk today? There's something I need to tell you." It's as though my throat is partly closed because the words come out breathy. My pounding heart doesn't help matters.

Without looking up, he says, "I don't know. I've got a lot on today, and apparently, so do you." His response is dry and emotionless.

"I understand, but I *need* to talk to you."

Harley leans against the counter and watches the exchange. I want Dad to be the first to know everything—not for sympathy, but so he is aware. He's my dad, after all, and once upon a time, I was his girl. Now I'm simply the stranger in his home, and he won't even give me the time of day.

"Maybe later." He rises, shuts his laptop, and walks away. He pauses in the doorway and turns back. "If you're planning to stick around, look for some horses that would be good to train and sell. Like you started doing before you took off."

I bite back what I really want to say and simply nod. I don't want to get into it with him this early in the morning. Heck, I haven't even finished my coffee. The time will eventually be right.

The front door clicks shut.

"Well, at least there wasn't yelling, and he acknowledged you," Harley says, a hopeful smile on his face.

"Yeah, I suppose."

"What do you want to talk to him about?" he probes.

"I want to talk to him first. Sorry." I shrug.

"No, don't apologize. You do what you need to. What are your thoughts on running the horse training and breeding program again? Like we were doing before you left." Harley grabs his boots and pulls them on.

"I'm not sure. I guess we can see how we go. I'm not planning to leave again, but other things may come up, and certain people may not want me here anymore, so I'm not committing to anything." I've got Olive under my feet now. She's a major factor in my decision-making. I worry that some of the family won't be welcoming to her, but who can hold her father against her?

"Sounds like a good idea. Let's get out of here and see what beauties we can pick up," Harley says, and I follow him out to his truck. He hitches up the horse float, and we're off, just like the good old days.

While Harley drives, I stare out the window. The sun has started peeking over the horizon. I've missed these mornings. The orange and yellow colors beam light across all the green, making it look brighter. Neighbors are out on their machines, getting an early start to the day while it's not hot. My phone chimes with a text.

"Who's sending you a message this early in the morning?"

Glancing at the screen, I say, "It's Isla. Just checking up on me." I laugh.

"Of course, it would be her, but she isn't an early morning person. Is she sick?"

No, she's babysitting my daughter who likes to wake at the butt-crack of dawn, is how I want to reply. Instead, I say, "I'm not sure. People change their habits."

I swipe and read her message.

> **Isla:** *It wasn't a great night. She was up every hour. How the hell do you do this on your own?*

> **Delilah:** *Oh, I'm so sorry. She's not usually that bad.*

> **Isla:** *She's grumpy and crying already. I don't think it's a good idea to keep her with me for another day. It's clear she wants her momma, someone familiar. I'm a stranger to her.*

I guess I won't get time to prepare my family. I can't leave her miserable with Isla. This is our first time apart except for when she was born, and I was in the hospital. Eli thought it best to keep her from me while I was healing and waiting. He was wrong.

> **Delilah:** *Okay then. Come around lunchtime. I'm not there at the moment. Harley asked me to go to the horse sales.*

> **Isla:** *Sounds like you're stepping right back into the job you left behind and loved.*

> **Delilah:** *You could say that. I spoke to Dad briefly this morning. It wasn't bad, but it wasn't good either. I think there's still a lot of hurt there.*

> **Isla:** *That's understandable. Maybe little Olive can start to change their attitudes.*

Delilah: *I hope so, or I'm going to end up homeless.*

Isla: *Don't be silly. You can stay with me if things don't go to plan, but I have a feeling they will work out how they're supposed to.*

Delilah: *Anything is an improvement compared to where I was a year ago.*

Isla: *That's true. You're already doing so much better by going home. I'll see you at lunchtime.*

Delilah: *See you then.*

"That seems like more of a conversation than a simple check-up," Harley says, giving me a sideways glance and then back to the road.

"You could say that." I pause, and while I had wanted to tell Dad first, it seems I'm going to run out of time.

I've got to tell someone about my daughter.

I may as well start with Harley.

Chapter 11

Delilah

TAKING A BREATH, I SAY, "I have to tell you something. I was hoping to have a little more time to prepare everyone, but it seems I don't." I rub my hands over my jeans. *How is he going to take this news?*

"What's going on, Dee?" he asks slowly and full of concern. "Is it about Eli?"

Swallowing, I continue, "No, it's not about him. That's for another time. I can't talk about him right now. It's… it's about my daughter."

Harley slams on the brakes.

My body jerks forward.

"What?" He maneuvers the car to the side of the road, puts it in park, then swings his body in my direction.

"I have a daughter."

Slowly, a smile grows on Harley's face. "I'm an uncle?"

"Yeah," I say slowly.

Harley releases a breath. "How old is she?"

"She'll be one in a month."

Harley takes off his cap and runs his hands through his hair and then down his face. "Wow, that's amazing, Dee. What's her name?"

"Olive." My throat swells as I say the word, knowing the meaning it has to our entire family. Mom was the glue for our family—she held everything and everyone together. I can't help but think what my life would've turned out like if she'd been here to guide and help me in a way that my dad couldn't.

"After Mom?" he asks. I don't miss the glistening tears in his eyes before he quickly wipes them away.

"Yes. No other name was as perfect. She's beautiful, Harley. I never wanted to keep her from the family. Other issues got in my way. Ones I don't w-want to dwell on." My voice cracks, emotion thick in the truck's cabin, it rolls around us in waves.

Harley leans over and pulls me into an awkward hug. "I can't wait to meet her."

"Good, because she'll be here about lunchtime today. I left her with Isla. She was telling me Olive had a bad night and isn't settling well." He releases me, and we settle back into our seats. I wish I could read his mind and know if he's genuinely happy for me or putting it on. On the outside, it appears he's happy.

"Okay, we'll make sure we're home by then. That's if you can stop yourself from buying too many horses," he mocks, knowing me so well. We once walked away with six horses, and they are still at the ranch being used for therapies and vacation guests.

I laugh, and it's as though a bit of the weight I've been carrying on my shoulders has lifted a little. Now to wait and see how the rest of the family takes the news of Olive. Especially Dad and Tally. "I'll do my best not to go too crazy."

"You're a mom. That's crazy, Dee. I'm sad that you kept it from us. We all would've loved to meet her."

"I know. Things weren't great at the time of her birth. There's so much more to it, and when I'm ready, I'll tell the family, but I think it's more of a pride thing right now. I don't know if I'm ready to admit that Dad was right about some things." He puts the car in drive, and we head off again, passing other homesteads that are still dark.

"You do realize Dad isn't going to hold anything in the past against you," he says cautiously.

I cock an eyebrow, turning to him as he focuses on the road. "You sure about that? Because it feels like he's doing that right now."

Harley releases a breath. "Dee, you left. We didn't hear from you for three years. We don't know anything about your life during those years. Let's drop the bomb of a baby in there now. It's a lot to take in. Some find it hard to forgive the silence, and that's the main problem. You could've kept in touch."

"I kept in contact with Sybil," I state. "I don't understand why it was all up to me to try to fix things or communicate. I was made to feel like the leper of the family… the black sheep. I had you and Hudson on Dad's side, and he basically slandered me because of my relationship with Eli. The girls were too afraid to offer their thoughts for fear of the same treatment. Now Tally is mad at me for the reasons you stated, but what was I supposed to do? Not even Sybil knows the full story of what happened when I left. Only Isla does because I wasn't afraid of her judging me." I stop before I drop everything onto his lap.

"Dee, when are you going to stop thinking we all hate you? It kinda shocked us that you've shown up out of the blue. We don't know what to think. Yes, Tally is a little more upfront about her feelings, but she's been stewing on these for the past three years. You closed yourself off to all of us."

"No, you all could've contacted me if you wanted," I snap a little more harshly than I intended.

"I guess we all could've done better, yourself included," he says gently. I immediately regret my outburst.

"Do you think they'll accept Olive? The rest of the family, I mean?"

"Why wouldn't they?"

"Because she's Eli's child, and I know he's no one's favorite person." I glance out the window and watch the trees and paddocks glide past us. We're close to our destination, and it can't come soon enough. This conversation has been hard, and even mentioning Eli's name out loud pains me in ways I can't fully describe.

"She's yours as well, Dee, and that's all that will matter to everyone. She's your daughter. Our niece and Dad's granddaughter. We'll love her no matter who her father is." He pauses for a moment as if contemplating his next words, then he finally says. "Dee, where's Eli? Does he know where you are?" He turns into the parking lot of the sale yards, puts the car in park, and turns to me a second time, weighed down by his gaze.

My throat clogs up, and I can't seem to put the words together. Pain and grief swell within me like rising floodwaters. "No, he doesn't."

"Are you in trouble? Is he coming to take Olive from you?" His fists clench around the truck keys, his knuckles turning white.

Shaking my head, I finally speak the words that I've not been able to for the past six months. "He's dead. He committed suicide."

Chapter 12

Delilah

SILENCE FILLS THE CAR AS another piece of weight lifts from me. Harley remains quiet. His mouth is slightly hanging open.

"I don't want to talk about it all right now. Can we go in?" What's weird is I'd expected to cry — to be this emotional mess when I told my family — and I'm not. I'm sad, but not in an all-consuming way. Eli was such a big part of my life, and I desperately needed out of that relationship, but I never expected him to be the one to end his own life.

"Oh, Dee, I'm so sorry." He reaches out and takes my hand, squeezing it.

"It's okay. I'm coming to terms with it now. He wasn't a good person, Harley. Not good at all."

He nods. "Well, I'm here if you want to talk about it."

"Thanks. Can you please not tell the rest of the family about Eli or Olive? When the time is right, I'll tell them."

"Sure, no problem." He gives me a half-smile.

"Telling you has helped ease the burden I've been carrying around with me for the last six months."

Harley squeezes my hand once more before releasing it. "You're home now, and we've got you. Let's go buy some horses. Nothing like shopping therapy to help ease the burdens on someone's mind."

We get out of the car and head inside.

I know he means well, and I'm sure he's right, but it will take time to heal. I'm still a single mother and learning to stand on my own two feet again. The time will come when one day, I'll close my eyes, and I won't see Eli in the state he was in. Until that time, I won't be fully okay. Admitting the truth about his death has helped, but only a little. Still, it's something and a step in the direction of healing.

After a morning of inspecting horses and watching them get paraded around, we've loaded up three horses that all need work, but I can fully see their potential. They haven't been well-taken care of and need green fields and lots of love and care, which I can supply.

"I think we did good," Harley announces as he slides into the driver's seat.

"Yeah, me too. Diamond is going to need some real TLC. She's afraid of us and a little wild. Did you see how she reacted when she was startled?"

"Yeah, quite jumpy. She'll be fine after some good care. She's beautiful," he says. Diamond is a gorgeous golden color with a brown patch shaped in a diamond on her head. She's stunning but skittish and unsure of people. It'll take some time, but I know she'll be a perfect beauty.

"I haven't really had a moment to walk around at home. Are things run the same, and do I still have some pens to work in, or are they used mostly for therapies now?"

"Um… I think we have the ones out near the holiday-stay cabins that we don't use. Perhaps we should use the small barn out there to keep these three in. That way, you've got some privacy to work with them."

"I'm going to have Olive to think about as well, remember?"

"Yeah, I know. I'm sure that between all the aunts and uncles and her grandad, she'll be looked after. You have to remember they're going to want to know her and be a part of her life now. I know I will, even if they don't. I'll strap on a carrier and cart her around with me. Maybe she can help me find a wife. I hear babies are chick magnets."

We both break out in laughter. "Why is that, and then when women are single mothers, no one wants the burden of caring for a child?" I state.

"Because the guys are losers or too focused on something else. They're the ones missing out." He shrugs.

"I'm resigning myself to the fact that it'll be me and Olive for the rest of my life."

"Don't talk like that. There's someone out there for you who'll care for you both."

"I'm not so sure. Who would want someone as broken as me? Trusting another man will be hard as well." Even the thought of opening my heart to someone else right now makes me cringe. I'm so afraid I'll end up in another similar situation like I was not that long ago. One I'm still healing from.

Harley throws me a quizzical glance. I bite my lip, realizing my mistake. "Why?" he asks.

My phone chimes with a message. *Thank goodness.* "It's Isla."

Isla: Hey, I'm almost at your place. Are you home?

Delilah: We're about five minutes away.

Isla: Yeah, same. I've just pulled over for a moment as Olive is not loving this car ride. Hopefully, she's okay when she's back with you.

Delilah: She'll be all right. I kind of need her anyway. I told Harley about Eli. Not everything— just that he committed suicide and he wasn't a good person. No big details.

Isla: I'm glad you told someone. I mean, I'm always happy to be here for you, but you need your family to help you through this harder part. I guess that's why I told a white lie to get you here.

Delilah: Don't worry about it. You're right. I can't do this alone. I need to be somewhere familiar with family. Even if some of them are still mad at me, and I'm not sure how to mend those fences.

Isla: It will all work out. Let them have their feelings, and eventually, you'll all move past it.

Delilah: I hope you're right because right now, there's only a handful who want me home or were happy to see me.

Isla: Stop reading into it. Focus on why you're there and heal. Let me know when you get to your driveway, and then I'll start driving. That way, you'll get there before we do.

Delilah: You can leave now because we're not far at all.

Isla: See you soon.

"Isla is almost at our place," I state as Harley turns the car onto the familiar road that leads to our house.

Harley reaches over and takes my hand, squeezing it. I hadn't realized I'd been wringing my fingers together. "It'll be fine, Dee. Everyone will love her."

"I hope so. Let's just get these horses off and then we can see how this is all going to go down."

"I'll get started," he offers and places his hand back on the steering wheel.

"I want to help. I don't need Dad thinking I'm slacking off because I've got a kid."

Harley sighs, rubbing his hand down his face. "He'll be fine. Stop thinking the worst. Things always have a way of working out."

I don't respond. I'm done talking for now. The things I have gone through are both physically and mentally draining. It's so much for my fragile heart. Now I'm raising my daughter on my own, and there will come a time when I have to explain things to her about her father.

The therapist I'd seen after Eli's incident told me that sometimes people feel like their families would be better off if they weren't here. I could've done without the abusive Eli, the Eli who liked to sling hurtful words at me to break me down as he did in so many ways.

I need to change my mindset and start thinking of Olive and doing better for her. Being home with everyone will help heal my heart. I'm sure of it.

Chapter 13

Sebastian

WHAT A DRIVE. IT WAS long, but thankfully, the girls are good with long drives. I pull into what looks like a makeshift parking area near a massive red barn. This place looks amazing—busy, that's for sure. I get out of the car, raise my arms over my head, and stretch. Dang, that feels good.

I take in my surroundings. It's as though a weight has lifted off my shoulders the minute I stepped out of the car. The hustle and bustle of the people around me, another giggling child catches my attention, her blonde curls in piggy tails. I admire the way her mother gets down to her level and inspects what made her laugh. The girl must be a year or two younger than Rylee. A pang of guilt and fresh pain shoots through me at an image of Anna-Beth doing this exact thing when Rylee was younger and throwing a tantrum. She'd comforted and soothed until Rylee was smiling again.

My name being called from the car catches my attention. I shake my head and open the back door, letting Rylee out and then go around and pull Ruby from her seat, resting her on my hip. "Come on. Let's go get checked in."

"Daddy, look... horses." Rylee points at a couple of workers who open a horse float and begin to lead a horse out of it. The horse appears to be quite rowdy and unsure of its surroundings. "Pretty horse."

"It is," I say as the golden horse stomps its hoof, stirring up the dust a little. The blonde woman attempts to soothe it while guiding it off. All of a sudden, the horse rears up, and with its front legs, hits the woman in her thigh. She cries out.

Taking Rylee's hand, I rush toward her, but before I get there, another worker has a hold of the reins and settles the horse. A man rushes over from the barn and takes the reins, leading the horse away.

The blonde woman hobbles to a nearby bench by the barn and drops onto it, inspecting her injury. I can't see blood or anything as I approach. I'm sure it'll leave a nasty bruise, though. It appeared to be a severe hit from the horse.

Before I get to her, a flock of girls and two guys all check on her. *Wow, they reacted quickly.* When I get within earshot, she's assuring them she's okay, and then her eyes land on me. Those familiar blue eyes bore into mine.

It's her — the woman from the hospital almost a year ago.

"You," I start.

Her eyes go wide. *Does she remember me, or was she out of it?* I wish I could've helped her that day. Her haunting face still pops into my head occasionally, and now here she is, though her hair isn't matted and messy. It's smooth and up in a ponytail. She looks so much better. The pale face I remember now has a pinkish tinge to her cheeks. "Do you remember me?"

Her face turns a brighter shade of pink. "I *know* who you are, but I'm not sure we've met. Surely, I'd remember meeting you," she says, and the people who came rushing to her stand back and watch the exchange.

"I helped you at the hospital about a year ago now. You wanted to get to your baby." I hear a sharp intake of breath from those around her. Sheer panic emanates from her wide stare.

"You were in the hospital?" A dark-haired woman whirls on her, and it's clear I've said something I shouldn't have.

She opens her mouth to say something when a crying baby draws everyone's attention. I glance down at Ruby, who's settled on my hip. It's not her. I turn to find another woman holding a baby with blonde hair and the same blue eyes as the mystery woman. The injured, unidentified blonde stands. *What was her name?* That horrid day rolls through my head again, and then it comes to me, Delilah.

A small, broken smile forms on her face. She winces as she puts weight on her sore leg and hobbles a few steps closer to me and then past me, taking the crying baby who settles instantly in her arms as she brushes her lips on the girl's head. Could this be the baby that she referred to in the hospital?

Delilah glances up at the group surrounding her all with wide eyes. "Yes, I was in the hospital. Yes, I had a baby. Family, meet Olive... my daughter."

There's a collective gasp.

Wow, okay. This feels extremely personal, and I need to leave.

I turn to walk away when Rylee puts on the brakes. "Daddy, can I say hello to the baby?" she says.

All focus is on us, then I catch Delilah's eyes, she nods and manages to lower herself down to a crouch so Rylee can meet her child.

Rylee, in her bright pink dress, hair in pigtails, wanders over with such confidence and is unaware of the tension rolling around within that circle. "Hey, baby," she coos. She's always been good with Ruby, helping to settle her. It's her caring nature. I'm sure that when they're older, there will be plenty of fights.

"What's your name?" Rylee asks Delilah.

She smiles at her with such vibrance I almost miss the glistening tears in her eyes. "My name is Delilah, but you can call me Dee, and this is Olive."

Rylee gently rubs her hand over Olive's head. Olive smiles and smacks at her. Rylee giggles. I take in those around me. They all have grins on their faces and tears in their eyes. There's a story here that I've walked into the middle of. I hope I haven't put my foot in it when I didn't mean to.

"Daddy, she's as big as Ruby. They can be friends," Rylee yells gleefully and races over, taking my hand and dragging me closer to Delilah. This is the first time in a long time I've actually taken notice of another woman since Anna-Beth.

Delilah appears to try to get up. I extend my hand. She stares at it a moment and then takes it as I assist her to stand. "This isn't exactly how we greet people here," she jokes, and I'm mesmerized by her beauty and strength. She's come so far from when I last saw her.

"That's okay. It seems I may have said something I shouldn't have," I whisper under my breath, hoping the people around us don't hear.

It's then I realize we haven't let go of each other's hands. Her skin is smooth. I glance down and notice some scars on the top of her hand. She gently removes it from mine and grips Olive tighter.

Delilah waves dismissively. "Don't worry about it. It was about to come out anyway."

"Excuse me, Mr. King?" one of the guys addresses me. I turn toward him. "Hey, I'm Harley. Welcome. If you'll come with me, we can get you and your family settled."

"Okay, sounds good. It was lovely to meet you, Delilah. I hope to see you around."

"I'll be here." She almost seems stunned.

"That sounds good."

"Daddy, can I play with Olive again?" Rylee asks, tugging on my free hand.

I take in her happy face. "I think Olive needs to get settled first, and then maybe we can catch up." My eye catches Delilah's and asks a silent question. She nods.

"I think Olive would love some friends to play with," Delilah says.

"Yay," Rylee cheers, clapping her hands.

"Come on, Rylee. We need to go find out where we're staying and let Ruby have a nap."

"Okay, Daddy." She wanders toward the door where Harley waits. With one last glance at Delilah, I smile and follow Rylee.

This woman. There's something about her that draws me to her. I don't know what it is. She's beautiful, that's for sure, but I don't feel any of the usual sexual impulses that pull a man toward a woman. It's something deeper, like the roots of an old tree dug into the earth. This woman, Delilah, has caught my attention and wrapped those roots around my heart, and I need to get to know her. I *want* to know more.

Chapter 14

Delilah

THAT WAS SEBASTIAN-FREAKING-KING, Formula One racer, and oh my goodness, he's even more attractive in person. Seeing him clutch his little girls put flutters in my heart. I take him in as he throws a quick look over his shoulder in my direction. He has black hair — I'd love to know what it feels like — and a heated chocolate swirl gaze. He gives me a small smile, and then his back is to me. He wearing some long beige pants with a nice-fitting white T-shirt. Wow!

"Hello? Earth to Delilah." Sybil's words pull me back under the bus where Sebastian threw me. It's not his fault. I remember a man helping me in the hospital. Everything from that time in the hospital is a blur. Surely, I should've known who he was. I'd been following his career all year. What are the chances he was at the same hospital as me almost a year ago?

"Sorry," I say, turning my attention back to Sybil, Mabel, Hudson, Talulla, and Odette. They're simply staring, their faces unreadable. I hobble forward, and a shooting pain runs up my leg and throbs. Sebastian's appearance must have momentarily taken away my pain. "This is my daughter, Olive. She's almost one." I turn to Isla, standing just behind me. I hope she can catch me if I fall because I've got no one else.

"I'm an aunty?" Talulla asks. The snide tone she'd been using with me previously is now gone.

"Yes, and I wanted her to know you all. I left her with Isla last night so I could prepare you, but it seems she missed her mom, and I couldn't let her be miserable."

"Can I have a hold?" Mabel steps forward with her arms out. The tears in her eyes tell me everything I need to know. She's happy. I take in Hudson, whose grin could brighten anyone's day, and Odette simply stands beside him. Tally and Sybil haven't moved, their faces are still unreadable.

"Sure, but she may not be happy. Isla told me she's been unsettled," I reply as Mabel comes closer. Olive watches her while snuggling into my neck, sucking on her pacifier.

"Hey, Olive, I'm your Aunty Mabel. You wanna come?" Mabel claps her hands. Olive eyes her and lifts her head to look up at me, those big blues a little unsure.

"It's okay," I encourage.

Olive's head moves back to my sister. Releasing her arms, she swings herself toward Mabel, who catches and takes her from me. My hand flies to my mouth. This moment isn't how I planned it, but it's more than I could have imagined as Olive lays her head on Mabel's shoulder and cuddles into her.

"Who baby?" Odette asks as she moves closer to Olive.

I come up beside her and take her hand, attempting to ignore the throb in my leg. "That's my baby, Odette. Her name is Olive."

Odette puts one of her fingers on her lips and starts chewing at her nail. Her nervous tic — it's as though she senses when there's tension surrounding her. "You have baby?" Her questioning eyes land on mine.

"I do." I smile encouragingly.

"She beautiful."

"Yes, she is."

"I say hello?" She continues to chew.

I reach up and move her hand gently from her mouth. "You can say hello. You're her aunty, after all." I'm not sure if she understands what that means, but at my words, she moves away from me and to Mabel, who's clutching a happy Olive.

Turning to the others, I ask, "Are you going to say anything?"

"You kept this from us for almost a year?" Tally's accusing tone is back, and it hurts. I don't want Olive to witness this.

"I'm not having another fight with you. You don't know the full story," I state firmly.

She crosses her arms over her chest. "You're right, I don't because *you* never told us. Never kept in contact. You kept something so important from us. It hurts, Dee. It really hurts." She takes off at a run toward the house, but I don't miss the hitch in her voice and the tears in her eyes.

I swing to Sybil. "I'm sorry I didn't tell you. There's so much I wanted to tell you but didn't know how." I wrap my arms around myself.

"You're going to have to give us the full story, but when you're ready, Dee. So many secrets. We're your family. You should feel like you can tell us anything."

"I wanted to tell you all, but I thought in person would be better, given the circumstances I left on. As it is, Tally is still angry at me, and who knows when Dad will talk to me properly… like hold a conversation properly. Do you think I'm enjoying the way I'm being treated by Tally and Dad? No, I'm not, yet Dad is the one who

drove me out, and Tally is holding it against me."
I step back.

My bad leg collapses beneath me, and I'm in
the dirt a moment later. "Dang it," I mutter.

Hudson is by my side in a flash. "Come on. We
probably need to get your leg checked out." He
helps me get back on my feet.

"No, it's just going to bruise. I wasn't ready
when I moved. It's fine." I dust my jeans off.
Mabel is cooing with Olive, who's smiling and
trying to hit her face.

Harley comes back into the circle. "So,
Sebastian is all sorted. Now I need a cuddle from
my niece." He moves to take her from Mabel,
who quickly runs off with her back to the
homestead. They all follow except Hudson and
Sybil. My stomach tightens. I should go with
them. I make a move, but then I hear Olive's high-
pitch giggle, and I pause. Perhaps a couple more
minutes will be okay before she becomes
unsettled.

Sybil rushes in and wraps her arms around
me. "I'm annoyed that you didn't tell me, but I
just hope you get to a place where you can open
up to us." She releases me. "Now, if you'll excuse
me, I need to get in line for a snuggle with my
niece." With that, she runs off toward the
homestead.

"I should go and talk to Tally," I say to
Hudson, who remains silent beside me.

He clears his throat. "I think you should leave her be for a little bit. She seems to be having a harder time than the rest of us with you coming back and now this." He gestures to the house.

"*This?* Hey, her name is Olive," I bite back.

He throws his hands in the air. "Whoa, take it easy. I didn't mean my words in a bad way. It's just a lot to take in." He removes his hat and runs his hand through his hair, then returns the hat back to his head.

"Let's get the rest of these horses out and settled. I wasn't planning on just bombing you guys with her. I did plan to tell you. There's so much more I want you to know, but maybe now isn't the time." I test my leg out and move to the back of the trailer again, where two more horses wait to be unloaded.

"Whenever you're ready, I'll be here."

I throw him a half-smile over my shoulder. "I know. I appreciate it. Now, let's get these boys settled. I'm going to have to put in some hard work with the girl. She's feisty. I might lead them down to the smaller training ring and barn. That way, they're not disrupting the other horses." I latch on the lead and move the black beauty out of the trailer. He's so tall but needs some work. "This one here is quite scared of people. It took a bit of coaxing to get him on the trailer. The other one seems like an anxious little thing, but he's beautiful as well. His molten colors are so different."

"They're stunners. Are we keeping these or planning to sell them?"

"That's up to you and Dad, I'm guessing. I'll do the work, and then you two can decide." The horse's hooves clack on the metal ramp, and once he's down, I hand the lead to Hudson and grab the other boy's lead.

"Well, I suppose we'll just have to wait and see how they go with training."

"Yeah, sounds like a good plan." I lead the other one out and then take the lead from Hudson. "Okay, I'll take these boys down to the other barn and then come back for the golden storm in there." I nod to the big red barn where the worker took Diamond earlier.

"I can take her for you," he offers.

"No, it's okay. I need a few moments to myself. Thanks, though."

"What about Olive?"

I give him a warm smile. "Trust me, if no one wants to cuddle her, Harley will, or Isla will take her."

"Does Isla know everything?"

I suck in and bite my bottom lip, then say, "Yes, she does because she never judged." I shrug.

Hudson nods, a sullen look passing over his features. "I get it. I suppose we all need to work on the communication side of things, yourself included."

"You're right with that statement." The black beauty jerks my arm as I grip the rope. "All right, buddy, let's get you settled. Okay, I'll be back shortly."

I head off down the dirt road toward a smaller barn where I used to work with the horses and train them. Did Dad close that one off as well like he did the library in the house?

Taking in my surroundings, I lead the boys. I forgot how big this place is. In my mind, it's small, but over the years I've been gone, so many new buildings and areas have popped up. There are people playing games on a grassy patch to the right of me and a barbecue area where a family is currently cooking up something that smells amazing. It causes my stomach to grumble. It seems as though the coffee has worn off.

After fifteen minutes or so, the little shack comes into view, and I'm suddenly whipped into the past. This was the first place I met Eli. He was only supposed to be passing through town but ended up staying. When I unhook the latch and pull the door open, the musty scent hits my nose. Nope, it hasn't been used.

I get the horses into a pen and come out to discover a pile of hay in one of the back corner stalls. It's fresh. Who would've put that there? I break one bale apart and throw it into the stalls, and I notice they have been cleaned recently as the water troughs are washed out as well. Was this Hudson's doing? Whoever it was, I owe them a thank you. It saves me some time.

I head out the back through the gate and into the training pen. It's clear it hasn't been used, but I'll change that. This ring is going to get a great workout with these horses. They have amazing potential.

"How's your leg?"

I whirl around to find Sebastian standing on the other side of the fence. A stabbing pain shoots up my thigh at the sudden movement, causing me to stumble but not fall, thank goodness. I don't need to embarrass myself on top of everything else.

"Are you all right?" He makes a move to climb through the fencing.

I quickly wave him away and hobble around until I find my feet. Stopping, I clutch my chest. "My goodness, don't sneak up on me like that. I'm not sure my heart could handle it more than once." I laugh and move closer to where he stands with his arms resting on the bar of the fence. I stop and put mine on the bar as well. He's even more gorgeous in person. In a racing suit, he's magic, but right here in front of me, it's another story. He sports the shadow of an unshaved beard. It's not long enough to be annoying, but it makes him look hotter than most of the men on this ranch.

He chuckles. "Sorry, I just saw you here. We're

staying over in that cabin, and I wanted to come by to make sure you were okay. My girls were tired, so I put them down for a nap and turned on the baby monitor." He holds his hand up, showing me a video of his girls asleep, one on a single bed and the other in a crib.

"Wow, they went down pretty quickly. I wish my daughter would do that." I straighten and smooth my hands over my torso, already feeling the heat of the day beneath my long-sleeve shirt.

"They're good girls. It's ah… taken me some time to figure it all out. So, how is the leg?" He clears his throat.

"Would it help if I said I completely understand? And my leg is fine. Thanks for asking."

He shrugs and stares down at his feet shuffling in the dirt, coating his black runners in a layer of dust. He lifts his head, and our eyes meet. "Is that man here with you?"

His question throws me. "Who?" I ask, my brow furrowed.

"When I helped you at the hospital, there was a man who came at me for helping and told me not to touch you."

Eli. That sounds like him.

"Oh, no. He isn't here." My throat swells with emotions. "I'm actually surprised you remember me because I must have been on some high dose painkillers that day and a little out of it that I don't remember you. I'm sure I'd recall being helped by a Formula One racer. I mean, I'm a huge fan, so I'm surprised I didn't jump on you," I joke and kick my boot in the dirt.

"You were in a bad way. You told me you were trying to get to your baby, and I think something about the guy not letting you see her."

"How can you recall something like that? That was a year ago."

His sad eyes meet mine, and then I know. It was the day he lost his wife. It was also the day I received a heart transplant because of complications from Olive's birth. My heart had weakened, and I'd needed an emergency heart transplant. Thankfully, I didn't have to wait long and because of the severity of the situation I went to the top of the list.

Now I think about it, the nurse told me I was very lucky because there was an organ donor who matched right away. I'd heard the nurses discussing an accident when I was lucid. *Could his wife have been an organ donor?* My mouth drops, but I quickly snap it shut. Surely not, no.

"That was the day Ruby came into the world, and my wife left it." His voice is low, but I don't miss the pained tone of his words. "I'm sorry. I don't even know you, yet here I am, talking about private things to you, and I don't know why."

"I'm happy to listen if it helps you."

"Maybe it's the fact that I helped you on the

day, and I couldn't help my Anna-Beth." His words catch, and he drops his gaze to the ground.

"I'm truly sorry for your loss. I… I know what it's like to lose someone."

We stare at each other for a moment. Nothing else around us matters. The birds singing in the large trees are all the noise we need at this moment. I've never had someone approach me and be so open and upfront. It's almost too good to be true that he'd show any interest in me.

"It seems those who are lost find each other when it's needed… maybe," he offers and rests his hand on my arm, which still leans on the fence. I don't make a move to pull away. It's good to have someone understand. He's known great loss just like I have.

Maybe we have something in common.

"Looks that way. I'd be happy to show you around one day. There's a children's area where parents can leave the kids and have a little time for themselves. My sister, Mabel, is the childcare worker and organizer of it all."

"Were those people who rushed to you your family?" he asks.

I nod. "Yeah, big family."

"That's really good, though. So, a family-run business here then?"

"You could say that. I mean, I only came back yesterday after being gone for a couple of years."

"Ah, now the whole baby situation makes sense." He grins as if having a light-bulb moment.

"What situation?" I frown.

He takes his hand from my arm and points up the road where we were only a moment ago. "When everyone was shocked to see your daughter. Was that their first time meeting her?"

"It was. There's a big story there." And an even bigger one between Sebastian and me if my calculations are correct.

"There must be. Anyway, I better let you get back to your daughter. I hope to see you around." He holds my gaze and gives me a mega-watt smile, causing my heart to stutter.

I turn back to the barn and head inside again, the entire conversation with him plowing through my mind. I can't help but wonder if he's here for a reason or not because if I'm correct in my assumption, then he might end up resenting me.

Could it be I was given Sebastian's wife's heart?

Chapter 15

Sebastian

THIS PLACE IS MAGICAL. BEING outside in nature with the trees, and the sounds of creatures and birds is one place I can really feel like myself and not have the weight of everything slamming down on my shoulders. Not the drama of trying to find a seat for next year or the drowning thoughts of the looming anniversary of Anna-Beth's death when I should be focusing on Ruby and her birthday.

I stop on the cabin's small front porch as Delilah limps back up the dirt road. Feeling like a fool, I open the door and step inside. The silence is deafening and painful. It's too quiet and makes me think way too much about Anna-Beth and her not being here to enjoy watching her girls grow up. Would we have had more kids? I wouldn't have been against it.

I just bared it all to a complete stranger. Well, not all, but I don't talk about my personal life with anyone other than family in case it's used against me in the media. That's the last thing I need right now. But Delilah seems different. It seems she protects herself and doesn't let people in easily. I was going to ask about who she'd lost, but again, it's not appropriate. I'm interested in getting to know her, though. A play date with the kids wouldn't be a bad idea.

I go straight for the refrigerator and see how full it is. On the website, the Rose Ridge Ranch staff asks for a list of things we'd like stocked in our refrigerators. It's a unique idea since many places don't offer this service. I didn't ask for much as I'd done a food shop when we passed through River Valley. We should be good for a while. I take a beer from the refrigerator and close it. I only allow myself this one and no more — it's my wind down while the girls sleep.

After heading through the back door to a bigger patio, I sit at the little table and stare out at the rolling green hills surrounding us. The barn where Delilah was is in clear view from where I sit. The sound of a running creek fills my ears along with horses' hooves clicking along the road. That's when I see her again. She's leading the horse that kicked her into the barn. She's so gentle and tries to pet the horse, but it rears its head back from her.

I'm not sure I could be so calm in that situation. Horses are big creatures with hard hooves. I don't fancy being stomped on anytime soon. If only people could hear my thoughts. I'm not scared of racing around a track at stupid speeds, but I'm afraid of a horse. That makes no sense.

My phone rings, and I grab it from my pocket before it can wake the girls. "Hey, Mom," I answer.

"How was the trip, honey? How are my beautiful girls?"

I rest back in the seat and take another mouthful of my drink before answering, "The trip was great. The girls are so good when traveling. They're asleep at the moment. They passed out the moment we got to the cabin."

"That's good. Do you need me to come help so you can have some time for yourself?"

"Mom, I can manage on my own for now. I'll let you know if I need help. Thanks, though. They have a kids' care thing here if I need some alone time. The entire place is nice. It's run by a large family."

"It sounds like a good vacation for you and at a good time with everything coming up." That's really why she wanted to come—to be here in case I needed her on that looming day. While I'm grateful to have a caring mother, sometimes she can be a little much.

"I know, Mom…" I pause, and before I can stop myself, I ask, "Mom, do you think it's crazy to be drawn to someone after only having met them briefly?"

"What do you mean?"

"There's a girl here, and I saw her at the hospital the day of Anna-Beth's accident. She wasn't in a good state at the time, and the man with her gave off a bad vibe. He wasn't very nice and came across as cold. Anyway, she's here, and I found myself comfortable talking to her and wanting to spend time with her. Is that weird and somehow wrong?"

"Oh, Sebastian, that poor girl. What's she doing there?"

"Her family owns this place."

"Oh, wow. Perhaps there's a reason behind you deciding to go. Things happen for a reason, Seb… that's what I believe. If you've met her before and there she is again… there's a purpose to it. Don't run from it, embrace it." Her words are gentle and hold so much meaning. I'm all for things happening for a reason, but it's still crazy when it happens.

"I'm not sure how to handle it. It's always been Anna-Beth, then the girls came along, and now it's them."

Mom laughs, and I'm not entirely sure why.

"What?"

"Seb, you don't need to rush into marrying this girl. Simply talk to her. No crazy stuff. Just look at it like making a new friend."

"Yeah, yeah, I know. Thanks for the tip, Mom, even though you made me feel like I was back in school." I laugh jokingly.

"Sorry. Well, I just wanted to check in and see how you and the girls were doing."

"We're good, thanks, Mom. I'll talk to you later." We end the call, and I go back to listening to nature's choir—the birds, the crickets, and the running creek. I glance in the direction of the barn again. She's outside simply walking around the pen, inspecting things. What's she planning on doing?

Her head turns in my direction, and our eyes meet. No words are spoken, but her piercing blue eyes burn into mine. There's something there, hurt maybe. What happened to her? Who did she lose? There are so many questions that I want to know the answer to.

I want to help lift the burden she appears to be carrying.

Chapter 16

Delilah

EVERY STEP TOWARD THE HOMESTEAD causes my pulse to increase, and now I can't get that thought out of my head. With each heartbeat, I'm wondering if it's Sebastian's wife's heart that's kept me alive and gave me life again so I could watch my girl grow up while she misses out on hers. It doesn't seem fair.

Voices filter out of the front door as I get closer. Not voices—laughter. I grin, pulling the front screen door open and stepping inside. To my left, my siblings are sitting on the floor with Olive crawling all over them. I stop and lean against the wall, taking in the scene. Even Tally has made her way out of the kitchen to watch and grin from the other doorway that leads back into the dining room. Babies seem to have this kind of effect on people and sometimes manage to bring them closer together.

Olive had brought Eli and me closer after finally healing from my surgery. During the process, something within him changed. He'd bring Olive to me, let me cuddle her, and let me be a mother. He was the Eli I fell in love with here on the ranch. Then he was gone within months. Losing someone to suicide causes more pain, hurt, and confusion. I blamed myself—still do in some ways. I keep replaying old conversations in my head like a broken record. Then I'd question myself. Did I say something that made him feel worthless? Did I do this to him?

Would I be here if Eli were still alive? I don't know. Probably not.

Mabel jumps up from her spot on the floor and rushes toward me, throwing her arms around me. I end up with some light brown hair from her ponytail in my mouth, so I pull it away. "She's beautiful, Dee. She looks like you but also has some of Mom's features." She pulls back, and her hazel eyes shine with unshed tears, causing mine to mist up.

"Thanks. It seems she's taken with you all." I nod in the direction of Olive. Tally races back to the kitchen from where she stood in the doorway. "I just wish I could figure one person out." I sigh.

"Don't worry about her, she'll come around.

She felt like you abandoned her when you left, and she had to try to move past that. It seems that you coming home has caused all those old feelings to resurface, and now she has to sort through them."

"Is there anything I can do to help?"

"Just be there for her. Chat to her like her mood isn't bothering you. That's hard, but I'm sure you can manage it." Mabel winks and turns to go back to the group.

Isla comes to my side. "This is going well," she whispers.

Folding my arms, I say, "Yeah, I guess the real test will be when Dad meets her. Has he come looking for everyone yet?"

"No, I asked Hudson, and he said that he had to go to town this morning. He must have left not long after you and Harley went to the horse sales, going on the information Hudson gave me."

"Come on. Let's get her things from your car, and I'll let you make your escape before things blow up," I half-heartedly joke. She nods, and we head back outside.

"How are you feeling about all of this?" She waves her hand around the entire ranch.

"I'm still processing. I think it's good for me. I need to heal, and working with the horses and having Olive be around the family feels right. Everything's kind of falling into place, even if some people here are still annoyed with me."

"Yeah, I'm sure they'll move past it eventually. Oh, my goodness, that was Sebastian King before, wasn't it?" The excitement in her voice rises a notch as we head to her car.

At the mention of his name, my stomach swirls. "Uh… yeah, it was. He actually approached me when I was putting the horses away out back."

She stops and grabs my arm, swinging me around to face her. "Tell me everything."

I fill her in on our conversation, and then I tell her about my thoughts on his wife. "I think my new heart came from her. I'm not a hundred percent sure, but I was really lucky because the day things spiraled for my health, there was an accident. I'd heard the nurses talking, and then I had a heart available to me, and even though the outcome was sad for the family of that person, I received my new heart from *an accident*. It was the same day his wife had her car accident. So, I'm kind of guessing, but it seems possible."

Isla's mouth hangs open. "You're kidding, right? Is there a way we can find this out?"

I shrug. "I have no idea, and I'm not sure I want to know. He's a really nice guy, and I don't want to invade his privacy. It doesn't feel right." We get to her car and start pulling Olive's bags and port-a-crib just as Dad pulls his car up beside hers and climbs out.

His gaze dances from our arms full of baby

stuff and then to the trunk of the car. "Hi, Isla, do you need a hand?"

She smiles. "I don't, but Dee does. This is all her stuff."

His brow furrows, but he comes over and collects the port-a-crib without saying another word.

Isla shuts the trunk, and we head back into the house. One-on-one therapy sessions are still going on, and I wish I knew how Dad would take to Olive. The cooing voices echo out to the porch, along with squeals of happiness followed by laughter.

We step inside, and Dad drops the crib on the floor by the door and stands in the doorway, staring at his family. I come up beside him and follow his gaze right to Olive.

"Dad." I walk over and pick her up. Her arms wrap around my neck, and I go back to stand in front of Dad. "This is Olive… my daughter."

Dad rubs his hand down his shirt and then over his face. His eyes don't leave Olive. Without hesitation and rather surprisingly, she leans out to him, her little hands grabbing hold of his shirt. I move to pull her back, but he takes her from me instead. Her little fingers find his face and smack at it. He tosses his head back to pull out of her reach. Then he comes back and pretends to munch on them. This makes her giggle, and tears fill my eyes.

This wasn't the reaction I was expecting. If anything, I expected him to take one look at her and walk right past her. I quickly swipe away the tears as they slip down my face.

"Olive, did you say?" he asks, without taking his eyes from her.

"Yes, after Mom."

"She looks like you as a baby, which means she also looks like your mother... spitting image," Dad says. Olive keeps trying to grab his face, which he pulls away from.

"Isn't she adorable, Dad?" Mabel steps up beside him, and it's like he just realized everyone's in the room. In a rush, he hands Olive back to me and then turns his icy gaze on everyone else.

"Do you all have something you should be doing? When I leave you in charge, I expect things to run smoothly," he barks as he takes off down the hallway toward the kitchen.

Hudson goes after him, I guess to try to smooth things over.

I grip Olive in my arms, and she begins to stir and get upset.

"Oh, don't worry, gorgeous girl. He'll come around," Mabel whispers before looking up at me. "She's beautiful. Thank you for bringing her home to all of us, so we can enjoy her as well. I'm happy to take her when you want to work with the horses."

"Thanks." I smile. "I might need that help. She's so used to having me with her all the time. I think it's good for her and me to have a little separation sometimes, but right now, I think I need to get her fed and down for a sleep. Did she sleep in the car, Isla?" I turn to my friend.

She shakes her head. "Like I said, she's been unsettled."

"That's okay." I nod to the bags Dad dropped on the floor when he arrived. "I'll get this set up, give her a bottle, and put her down." I hoist Olive on my hip and move to grab the cot, but Harley beats me to it.

"I'll help. After all, I've already missed out on a year of her life. I don't want to miss anymore."

"She's not one yet… she will be in a week."

"Oh, my goodness, we can throw her a party," Sybil announces, and they all murmur their agreement. "Maybe Tally will bake her a cake."

It's then I notice her back in the doorway. Our eyes connect, and she gives me a tight smile and nods.

"Thank you," I say. "Now, let's get her to bed, or she will be horrible later on."

After finally getting Olive to settle, I ask Sybil to keep an ear out for her so I can go down and check on the horses. She was more than happy to. I forgot how good it is to have family surrounding me. I walk past Isla, who's walking with Hudson. She's flirting with him — I wonder if he even notices it. She's paying too much attention to what he's saying and giggling while playing with her hair.

"Hey, Isla, what are your plans?" I inquire. She says something to Hudson and then heads in my direction.

"Hey," she greets me. "I think I'm going to head back. If you need me, I'm always a phone call or a message away."

I pull her into a hug. "Thanks so much for being my constant support and friend over the years. Most friends would've abandoned me long ago. I appreciate your friendship."

She squeezes me. "I've got your back. Always have, always will."

We release each other. "When will you leave?" I ask.

"Now seems like a good idea, I think."

"I'm just heading down to the horses. So thanks again for everything. I'll message and let you know how things go."

Her eyes brighten. "And you need to keep me informed if anything happens with the spunky racer guy, Sebastian."

I shake my head, smiling. "Nothing is going to happen there."

Her hands go to her hips, and she gives me a

pointed glare. "Just see what does or doesn't happen. Be open to possibilities."

"Yeah, yeah, whatever." We say our goodbyes, and she climbs in her car and heads off. I turn in the direction of the little barn.

With my head down, I make my way to the stall where I left the three beauties we picked up this morning. Their whinnying sounds off as I approach. I still need to go and see Holly. Knowing her, she'll probably nip me to tell me she's mad at me.

Cute giggles catch my attention, and I follow the sound. Before I can catch myself, I have a little girl wrapped around my legs.

"You're the horse lady," she states perfectly. Her hair is in two braids on either side of her head — it has changed since I last saw her chatting with Olive.

"Oh, hello, you." She clings to me, so I maneuver my way out of her embrace and squat down to her level. "What are you up to?" She wraps her arms around my neck.

"Rylee, you probably shouldn't do that to strangers."

My chest flutters as Sebastian comes to a stop in front of me. I take him in from knee height. He grins down at Rylee and me while clutching a wiggling Ruby in his arms.

"We're not strangers. We met before. She has a baby the same size as Ruby," Rylee announces as I rise from my spot. Rylee reaches out, takes my hand, and swings it back and forth, a big cheesy grin plastered on her face.

"I do have a baby the same size as Ruby."

"Where is she?" Her curiosity makes me smile. I love how innocent kids are—they're pure and bring such life and light into some of our darkest moments. Olive has been my lifesaver.

"She's asleep, so her Aunty Sybil is listening out for her while I check on the horses I bought today. Do you want to come with me?" I sneak a peek at Sebastian, who remains silent throughout the conversation. This isn't how I imagined meeting someone famous. Having a total fangirl moment wouldn't be appropriate, but the pounding in my chest tells me there's more to him than his superstar career. The way he speaks to me and the gaze we shared across the field today while I did the horses—it shook me. I mean, it's not right. I've lost Eli recently.

"Daddy, can we go see the horses?" Rylee grips his hand and tugs on it.

"I don't know. We don't want to put Dee out."

I wave my hand. "No, it's okay, but you can't come into the pen with these ones as they aren't trained well yet. That's what I'm going to do... train them so they can go to a new home or be used here on the ranch so that other people can ride them."

"Let's go see the horses," Rylee shouts, and

Ruby squeals, flailing her arms in the air. He chuckles. Rylee grips my hand, practically dragging me alongside her. Is this what I have to look forward to with Olive? Her dragging me around every which way she wants? Heck, I'd do anything for that girl. She can drag me anywhere if it means I can keep her safe from the badness in the world.

The silence between Sebastian and me is filled with a chatting Rylee asking me about the horses. "Is this the one who kicked you?" she chirps and skips beside me as we pass the golden beauty in her stall.

"Yes, it is, but she only did it because she's scared. She hasn't been well looked after and needs some training and love."

"Does your leg hurt?" Sebastian asks.

"Not really, but it has a wicked bruise appearing on it. I checked it before putting Olive down, and it's already coloring." Only because I bruise easily. Eli knew this, and when he didn't want me going anywhere, he'd cause some pain and up would pop a bruise I didn't want anyone to question. I shake my head to rid myself of the memory and return to the present, where Rylee asks another question.

"What's its name?"

"Her name is Diamond. She has a diamond-shaped brown patch of hair on her head. I'll show you when we get there."

"That's a pretty name," Rylee says and then falls silent. My gaze shifts from her to Sebastian, whose focus is on me. My cheeks warm at his intense look.

"You okay?" he asks.

I nod. "I am."

"You went somewhere a moment ago. I noticed you drifting off." He tilts his head to the side and studies me.

"I'm fine. Just a memory I'd rather forget."

"Want to talk about it?"

"I'm not sure I'm ready for that conversation yet. Well, not with a complete stranger. I don't want to scare you off," I joke and then fall silent. The sounds of other families and support workers talking among each other and their clients go on around us as we head down to the barn.

"I'm not sure anything would scare me off, to tell you the truth. I'm a little shocked with myself at how easy I find it to talk to you... a complete stranger. Usually, I'm a pretty private person." He fusses over Ruby in his arms and hands her a cookie from a snack bag he's carrying. She snatches it from his grip and puts it right in her little mouth eagerly.

I grin as she attempts to eat it. Well, suck on it. "Why me, though?" I blurt out, not really thinking. *Stupid question, Dee.* I want to smack myself in the forehead, but Rylee gripping my hand reminds me not to make more of a fool of myself.

"Honestly, I'm not entirely sure myself. From the minute I met you, I've wanted to talk to you, get to know you. Don't worry… I'm not seeking anything other than your company and even now, as I listen to myself speak, I sound like a fool. Please feel free to ignore me and my ramblings."

I laugh, and a lightness fills my chest. The memory that was there evaporated. Sebastian caused it to go away with those few words. "It's okay. It's good to have someone to talk to, and maybe it's because we both have kids around the same age that you're comfortable with me. It's easy talking to other parents because the conversation is mostly about the kids and not much else. I'm not too keen to share my 'much else' information. My family doesn't even know it, which is kind of sad."

"If you don't mind me asking, why did you leave here in the first place?"

This isn't where I wanted the conversation to go, but I answer him anyway. "I fell in love with the wrong person, and now I've basically come back with my tail between my legs."

He leans back and says, "There's no tail, is there, Rylee?"

Her head swivels in my direction, and she shakes her head. "Humans don't have tails, silly." She giggles, and it's a song for my wounded heart. That little sound brings me so much joy.

"Of course not. I know that," I respond and throw Sebastian a playful glare, shaking my head.

"Sorry. Just trying to get a smile out of you."

"Oh, you've done that all right." I smile.

"How was it with your family meeting Olive?" He shuffles Ruby to his other hip.

"They seem happy, apart from two of them, but I'm not sure what I can do about that. I'm trying my best." Even while I'm holding myself together with tape, it doesn't seem to be working very well.

"I'm sure you are. They'll come around eventually."

"I hope so. I still wonder if I should just leave again."

"Don't leave things where they are. You never know when or if it'll be the last moment you have together."

I turn to face him. Our eyes lock, and that pull toward him tightens as he becomes vulnerable right in front of me. Tears well in his eyes, but he quickly blinks them away and faces forward again just as we arrive at the barn.

Rylee releases my hand and runs for the barn door. Thankfully, she can't get into the stalls. Without thinking, I reach for Sebastian's hand and take it in mine, giving it a gentle squeeze. No words need to be exchanged — we understand each other at this moment.

"Come on," Rylee yells from inside the door. Instantly, I release his hand and follow her little voice. "This one is kicking the wall," she says, pointing to the closed half door on the stall.

"That's Diamond. She needs to settle in a little bit. Can I pick you up and show you?" I ask.

"Yes, please," she replies. I hoist her onto my hip, and her breath catches when she spots Diamond dancing around her stall in circles, throwing her head up and down. "She's so pretty."

I glance down at Rylee, her eyes wide with excitement as she grips the door with her little hands. "She is, and once she's trained, she's going to be even more amazing."

"Can I see the others?"

I lift her higher on my hip, and we go about checking on the two boys. Rylee isn't as interested in them as she is in Diamond. Sebastian remains silent, following us around and agreeing with anything his daughter says or asks.

Rylee runs out into the training pen. She can't run off anywhere unless she climbs through the bars. Sebastian, as if reading my mind, moves to the doorway so he can keep an eye on her. I hang back a moment and soak up this scene. Back when I'd been a girl making out with the farmhand in the barn, I'd imagined this future for Eli and me—a child racing around the pen as we watched on.

"You know, you're doing an amazing job with your girls. I'll admit that I've missed watching you on the track, but watching you with your girls? I get why you needed time," I remark as I move closer to him.

Sebastian turns. The shadow of his beard makes him that much more appealing, and his penetrating dark eyes hold mine. I'm sure he'll have no problem finding another wife when the time is right for him. "Thanks. My mom has been the biggest help. I'm not sure I'd have survived if it wasn't for her. Raising a newborn isn't easy, and then throw in a five-year-old, and it's a party." He turns back to Rylee, and I come up beside him.

"I totally get it. I'm just going to try to work with Diamond a little. You're welcome to stay if you want."

"Thanks. I'll let her play, and I'll attempt to keep you company."

Talking with him is so easy. I shouldn't feel this comfortable with someone so soon—it's not even been a day—but it seems we've somehow found comfort in each other over our broken pasts. How is it that two damaged souls like us could find each other, both suffering a loss? Maybe people like us gravitate toward each other without realizing it, perhaps to help each other heal.

I go to the cupboard where there's a heap of my old training gear, plus some new things I've not seen before. I take a blanket and grip it. Turning back to Sebastian, I find him watching me. His eyes drop, and then I see it—the scar from my transplant peeking out of the top of my shirt. I readjust, and it falls back into place, covering the scar. My heart hammers in my chest, the nerves are taking hold. *Please don't ask.*

"What happened there?" He points to his own chest.

"Oh, nothing." I'm not good at this deflection business. You can't miss a scar like that on someone.

"Did you have surgery?" he probes again.

"You could say that." I keep moving toward the stall where Diamond is and lay the blanket on the door. I don't plan on putting it on her. I just want her to see that it's not harmful in preparation for when it does go on her.

"Sorry, I didn't mean to pry. It's just not many people I see who've had what looks like open-heart surgery at your age. I mean, I know it's possible because bad things happen. It's okay if you don't want to talk about it. I was curious, that's all."

My hand hovers over the latch. I pause and hang my head, releasing a breath. "Yes, I had surgery almost a year ago now. I'm okay, though, and I'd much rather not talk about it as it's really hard for me." Yep, I'm going with that line. It's the last thing I want to talk about with him or anyone if I can help it. I'll have to be more mindful of how my shirts sit from now on.

"That's okay. I didn't mean to upset you."

"It's fine." Without another word, I unhook the latch and step into the stall. Diamond eyes me while moving from side to side, throwing her head back and moving in a jittery fashion.

I hold my hand out. "Hey, girl. You're okay. You're beautiful, aren't you? I'm not going to hurt you." I gently talk to Diamond, wanting her not to only feel but see that I'm not going to hurt her.

She stops moving and watches me. I hold her gaze, but she turns away and goes into a circle. I stay standing in there with her, not moving, simply watching, silently wishing Sebastian hadn't seen my scar. Will he make the same connection I did? Not that I even know if it's true or not. Secretly, I hope it's not true. I'm not sure how I could process that bit of information—that I have his wife's heart.

"Will she eventually calm down and come to you?" Sebastian's soft words startle me. A trickle of unease slides over me, slowly increasing to a wave. I don't know why. He seems like a great guy, and his girls are beautiful, but what's this feeling I'm suddenly beginning to have for him—this invisible pull? It's crazy and not something that normally happens. Well, not to me anyway.

In a whisper, I say, "It will take some time for her to be calm with me. Maybe a couple of days when she sees I pose no threat to her. She's had a bad life by the looks of it."

"How old is she?" he asks.

"She looks young, but I'll have to get the vet to come take a look and examine her when she's settled in a little." I hold my hand out to Diamond again. She stops and then throws her head back and turns away from me. I drop my hand by my side and wait.

"It all sounds like a lot of work."

"It is, but it's something I'm good at... working with horses. I've actually missed it and being back here feels right like it's healed a small part of my damaged heart." My cheeks heat at my honesty. I can't help it. Why does my guard drop with him? It's not natural to be this comfortable with someone so soon. "Sorry, I probably shouldn't have said that. I'm sure you don't want to hear about my problems."

"It's fine. I'm sorry to hear that." I'm glad he doesn't say anything else.

I don't respond. Keeping my mouth shut is the best thing right now. I never want to become a vulnerable person again. I gave so much of myself to Eli that I fear I had lost the person I was before he came along. I fell head over heels so quickly that whenever I think back on that time of my life, I know I was so stupid for being such an easy target for someone like him. People like Eli know how to make a girl feel special, loved, and wanted in the beginning as if they're setting a trap for them.

After some time, I make one last attempt with Diamond. With a sigh, I leave the stall and spot Sebastian in the training pen, leaning against the fence and staring down at his girls happily playing in the dirt. A small smile plays on my lips, and a swell of adoration builds in my chest. He has his girls. They mean everything to him, and I can't allow my stupid feelings to grow.

They're fangirl feelings.

They have to be.

Chapter 17

Sebastian

SENSING HER EYES ON ME, I keep my focus on the girls for fear of scaring her away. She has this runaway vibe about her, and I don't want to cause her to feel unsettled or uneasy with me. It's not my intention. The mention of her scar unsettled her — that was clear.

"Daddy, can I have horse-riding lessons?" Rylee's sweet words choke my heart. We've always been city people. For her to have the courage to try riding a horse brings me so much joy. *Anna-Beth would be proud.*

"We can look into it, Ry."

"Can she teach me?" Her finger dashes out, and she points to Dee, who has moved and is putting the blanket back from where she got it.

"I'm not sure she'll have time. She has a baby and will be training these horses."

"Please, Daddy? I like her. She's kind."

"She is," I agree. "How about we ask, but if she says no, then the answer is no, and we'll ask someone else. Okay?"

"Yes, Daddy." She jumps up and dusts off her clothes. I collect Ruby, who's covered in dust, but it's good for her to explore and try new things, even if that's eating a little dirt. *Anna-Beth would've freaked out.*

Rylee skips over to Delilah and takes her hand again. "Can you teach me to ride a horse, please?" Her big eyes stare up into Delilah's, and Delilah's smile falters a little but then corrects itself into something so beautiful it steals my breath.

"What does your dad say?" She drops down to her level, something Anna-Beth used to do when talking with Rylee. She found she held her attention longer when she gave her full attention to our daughter.

Rylee bounces on one foot and then the other as though she needs to use the bathroom, but I know it's her pure excitement. "He said only if you say yes, or I have to go with someone else."

I rub my hand over my face. Too honest for her own good, that one. "I only said that because you've got your daughter and training these horses, and I'm not sure what else with running a place like this. So, it's all up to you. I don't want to put you out—"

I'm cut off by loud laughter from Delilah and Rylee's little giggle.

"What's so funny?" I ask.

Delilah stands, pulls her phone out, and then faces it in my direction. I grimace when I see myself with brown dirt smeared over my face. I glance down at my hand, and it's covered in dirt. Must be from dusting off Ruby's bottom.

"You've got a great look going here." Delilah chuckles, her phone still on me as she snaps away. "This'll look good on social media, don't you think, Rylee?"

"Daddy needs a shower." Her high-pitched giggles cause me to laugh. Within seconds, we've all got tears streaming down our faces.

"Now it's turning to mud," Delilah offers, then reaches out and wipes her hand on my cheek. "I think I made it worse," she says breathlessly as I take in her proximity. She's close, so close. As I reach up to wipe my face, our hands collide. I take her hand in mine, pull it down, and keep a light grip on it. The thrumming in my chest turns into a pounding in my ears. The warmth of her touch is soothing yet frightening at the same time.

I release her. That was too much from me, too soon. "Sorry."

"That's okay." She lifts her hand and swipes away a few strands of her blonde hair. She's so beautiful. Those big blue eyes hold mine for a beat, and then she smiles. "I'd be happy to give Rylee some riding lessons while you guys are here."

I shrug. Ruby's little hand slaps me in the face, removing me from the trance I was in. I jerk my head back and move her hand away. "Only if you have time. I'd hate to put pressure on you and your family."

"That's okay. I'm sure I can make time for you both. Every girl should be taught to ride a horse if they want to. I remember when my dad first put me on one. I was so frightened and even got kicked off a few times, but you always have to get back on if you fall off." She shrugs.

I open my mouth to respond when her phone rings. Pulling it from her jeans back pocket, she says, "Sorry, it's my sister who's watching Olive. I have to get this."

I nod, and she answers, "Hey, Sybil, is everything okay?" She's silent for a beat and wipes her hand over her face, tiredness evident in her eyes. "Okay, I'll be there shortly." Ending the call, she sighs and then glances in my direction. "Sorry, I have to go. It seems Olive is rather unsettled." Another sigh.

"That's all right. I should get these two back home for baths and find some dinner. I can give you my number, and you can message me when you have some free time if that works for you?" I offer.

"Sure, not a problem. Here, I'll give you mine as well so you know it's me." We exchange numbers and say our goodbyes as we exit the barn and leave the horses be.

"I like her, Daddy," Rylee says as she happily takes my free hand and swings it back and forth while we walk to our cabin.

"I like her too," I admit to my five-year-old.

"I can't wait to ride a horse."

"What will you do if something bad happens? Will you ride again?" I ask, wanting to make sure she understands that this adventure may not go to plan.

"She said that if you fall off, you have to get back on, so I'll do that."

My heart swells with pride. Rylee will be a force to be reckoned with later in life.

We fall silent. I take in the trees and hills surrounding us and the sun beginning to dip behind them. Our first day here is coming to an end. It's going to be amazing, and I can't wait for what's to come, especially with Delilah working close to the cabin.

Seeing her would brighten anyone's day—especially mine.

Chapter 18

Delilah

OLIVE'S UNSETTLED CRIES STIR ME awake from a deep sleep. I groan and reach over to my bedside and turn the lamp on. Getting up, I stumble a little. She has been unsettled for the last four days. These sleepless nights are killing me. She was fine until we came here. I know she'll settle eventually, but I guess with so many new faces and less time with me, change is taking its toll on her. Tomorrow—well, today—I'll spend more time with her and take her for a walk around the farm to see all the different animals, and maybe even take her to some places where her dad and I would hang out together.

Olive stands in her crib, clutching the side and bouncing while crying. I hope she's not waking the house up. I pick her up and warm the bottle beside my bed. This little bottle heater is a lifesaver. I don't have to go to the kitchen to heat bottles anymore. Best money I've ever spent.

I glance at my phone. It's five-thirty. Please go back to sleep, Olive, I silently beg, already knowing my chances are slim of getting any more sleep. An early start is for the best. I can get as much done as possible while Olive sleeps.

Her little squeaks as she gulps down the last of her bottle bring a smile to my face. She's mine, my beautiful Olive. I still find it hard to believe sometimes that I actually have a baby. I survived some of the most challenging years of my life to end up back here, in this same house full of memories—some good and some bad. I survived a failing heart only to be given a second chance at life, to be able to raise this little girl.

My arms tighten around her, and an immense swell of happiness and love fill me so much that I'm sure I'll burst. The love that a mother holds for their child is so special, and my heart breaks for Sebastian's girls, who miss out on those mother-daughter moments. It's not fair. Life's not fair sometimes.

Olive finishes the bottle. I remove it from her mouth, and her tongue keeps on sucking gently. I lift her slowly as if she's a stick of dynamite that might explode with a sudden jolting movement.

After placing Olive back in her crib, I tiptoe

downstairs. My feet stop once I see the light is on in the kitchen. I could go back up, but I find myself moving forward, carrying me down the hallway and into the lit room. Once again, Dad sits at the table with an iPad, a cup of coffee, and a plate of food.

"Morning," I mumble and make my way into the kitchen to get myself a cup of coffee. I'm going to need an IV, given the state Olive has been in lately. I've heard it takes a few nights for babies to settle into new places and new routines.

"Morning," Dad responds. "Rough night?"

My hand freezes while grabbing a mug from the cupboard. I shake my head. "Uh, yeah. Olive still isn't sleeping well, so I'm not either, which makes it hard for me to get to the horses." I turn and notice his eyes still trained on the screen in front of him, so I go back to my coffee.

"You could leave her with Mabel in the childcare? As much as it's for the camp stayers, it's for the workers as well," he offers before taking a sip from his steaming mug.

I finish making my drink and sit opposite him at the table. "I could. I'm just worried she'll continue to be upset."

Dad peers over the top of the iPad. "Delilah, kids are resilient. She'll be upset for a short time but will be fine. She'll have fun."

"I know. I think it's me who has the problem with leaving her, even if it's with her aunty. I have no doubt Mabel will dote on her and carry her around all day just to make her happy." I laugh at the thought of her doing just that. "Olive would love that. I wouldn't, though, because that's what she'll come to expect... to be carried everywhere."

Dad's silent a moment before saying, "Let them dote. They want to get to know her since she's already nearly a year old, and they feel like they've missed out on seeing her grow." His voice cracks, but he clears his throat then goes quiet.

I take a sip, swallow, and then say, "I know I've denied them something by bringing her here too late, but I'm not sure everyone understands my circumstances and what I've been through this past year." *I will not cry. I will not cry.* Dad is finally talking to me, and if tears become a part of the conversation, he'll most likely tap out. He never was good at dealing with girls and their emotions, no matter how much Mom tried to help him.

This time, he places the iPad down in front of him, and his dark eyes meet mine. "You're right, we don't, but that's not our fault. You kept your distance." His calm and even voice startles me. A part of me expected yelling and that we'd end up having a screaming match.

"I did because I thought everyone here was mad at me. I've found that's not the case anymore."

"It's been years, so they've had time to think about things." He pauses, glances down at the table, and then back up. "I realize I said some horrible things, and I guess I'm angrier at myself for driving you away instead of loving you. Maybe if I'd done better, you wouldn't have kept Olive from us and maybe would've come back from time to time." His eyes glisten as tears well, but he furiously blinks them away. Always the conservative one.

Clearing the thick emotions from my throat, I say, "Dad, I'm not sure I would have. Eli wasn't the person I thought him to be." I dab at the wetness in the corner of my eye with my shirt. Admitting this to him is at the top of the list of hard things for me to do. "I just want you to know that you were right. Would I change things if I could go back? I don't know because now that I have Olive, I don't think I could ever give her up." I choke out the words. The thought of not having her in my life upsets me.

"What do you mean?" His salt and pepper brows furrow.

I open my mouth to respond when Mabel comes in, stumbling as though she's half-asleep. She even bumps into the counter. "Ow..." she mumbles and goes right for the coffee machine.

My eyes travel back to Dad. "I guess we'll finish this later. I was planning to clean up the library at some stage. Would that be okay with you?" I take another sip and savor the rich flavor.

He nods. "Sure, sounds good." He even

manages a half-smile before rising from his spot and washing out his cup, then nods good morning to Mabel before leaving the house. He's most likely going to his office in the big barn.

"Sorry, I didn't mean to interrupt," Mabel says, her hair in disarray as she walks around in her Sailor Moon pajamas. It was one of our favorite shows as kids. Us girls used to pretend to be the Sailor Scouts.

"That's okay. I'm sure he was ready to leave any minute." I take a long sip of my lukewarm coffee.

"At least you two were talking. That's a good sign."

I shrug. "Yeah, it's good. Not sure if we got anywhere, but it's a step in the right direction." We fall into a comfortable silence before I remember Dad's suggestion. "Do you think I could leave Olive with you for a couple of hours this morning while I work with the horses? I haven't been able to do much with them since Olive has been so unsettled. I guess I'm asking for some help." I offer a weak smile.

Her eyes go big and bright as if she's just won the lottery. "Oh, my goodness, yes, of course, I'll watch her."

"Thanks." I laugh.

"I'm just so glad we get to know her. She's very much your daughter, but I can also see bits of Eli through her. Will he be coming here?"

I shake my head. "No, it's complicated, but he won't be in our lives anymore."

"What do you mean?"

I need to hold a family meeting, so I can tell them all at once instead of one at a time. "How about I tell you tonight at dinnertime? That way everyone is here, and it will just be easier." The thought of telling them about Eli causes my stomach to knot within itself and my heart to pound, setting me on edge. It was hard enough to tell Harley, but I'll feel better once it's done and they're all aware of what's happened.

"Is it that bad?"

"Depends what you define as bad. Eli wasn't a great boyfriend, and it took me a long time to figure that out."

"I'm sorry, Dee. I'm sorry it didn't work out how you planned."

"Maybe I'm not meant to find happiness in loving someone. I'm not sure I'd be able to trust the next person so easily."

Mabel screws her face up. "No, don't think like that. Everyone deserves happiness, and it all comes in its own time. Just because Eli wasn't what you expected doesn't mean the next guy will be as bad or even bad at all."

Swirling my finger around the rim of my mug, I stare at the dark liquid. "I'm not sure how to trust someone again."

"You will. Trust me. I've noticed the race car driver eyeing you off when you're not paying attention."

My head shoots up, and her eyebrows waggle. "I don't believe you. He's too focused on his girls and most likely his career to have time for anything else, especially dealing with a broken woman like me."

"Dee, you've been so focused on Olive that you haven't seen what I have even from a distance. Over the last couple of days, he's dropped off his youngest daughter, Ruby, and you'll walk by, and his eyes will follow you. I'm telling you, jump on that, even if it's temporary. Go in with the attitude of just having fun. No harm can happen that way."

"You're not a matchmaker, Mabel. Perhaps he was watching someone else." Even as I say it, I hope he was watching me, but surely, I can't trust my feelings right now. I remind myself it's just a stupid fangirl crush.

"No, he asked me about you."

Oh, no. What did he say to her? I told him that I'd lost someone. Did he tell her that? Is that why she's probing about Eli?

"What did he ask?" The words rush out.

She giggles. "He wanted to know if you were single… he knew I was your sister. He said you'd told him that it was a family-run ranch and that I run the vacation care."

"He didn't," I scoff. "Now you're playing games with me."

She stands and stares down at me. "Believe what you want, but I told him that I wasn't sure what your relationship status is at the moment and to ask you himself."

"That's a little harsh, don't you think?"

"No, I didn't have an answer for him. So maybe have a chat with him. He could introduce you to your future someone. You never know what's around the corner in life." She's always the free spirit with all the positive vibes to get through the day.

Mabel takes her cup with her and exits the kitchen, and I'm left in silence as the sun slowly creeps up. It's the start of a brand new day—a new beginning. Tonight, my family will know the truth about my past, and hopefully, that will help me heal a little more. I'm a patchwork quilt in the process of being fixed.

Only time can heal me—time and just being here with family.

Chapter 19

Delilah

STANDING OUTSIDE THE LITTLE VACATION care granny flat we have, I grip Olive in my hands. She wasn't great for Isla. What if she's just as bad with Mabel? Have I conditioned her to only want me? There wasn't much I could do about that, considering it's only been her and me since Eli died.

"Are you planning to stand and stare at the building all day?"

Whirling around, I come face to face with Sebastian, Rylee, and Ruby, all bright-faced and grinning.

"Hey there. Yeah, I'm deciding if I want to take her in today or not. She's not been herself lately." I can't take my eyes from his—they captivate me in a way Eli's never did. There's a tenderness in his gaze. Maybe even some vulnerability.

"Well, perhaps we could do it together? Rylee wants to hang with Ruby today in here for a little while, so I'll have a little time to myself, and I'm not sure what to do."

I take in the beautiful girls. Rylee's hair is up in a high ponytail. She holds onto Ruby's foot, which dangles by Sebastian's hip. Ruby rubs her eyes, and I smile at her, which she returns. She's the same age as Olive, give or take a few days.

"Let's get this over with, and maybe, if you're interested, I can show you around," I offer, even though my entire body is trembling at the idea of hanging out with a guy again, just him and me, for the first time since Eli. Am I betraying him because it's only been six months?

"Sounds like a good idea." His words snap me from my worrisome thoughts.

Sebastian makes the first move toward the front door, and I follow. The moment I step in, I want to run back out and just cart Olive with me everywhere. I felt the same when I left her with Isla, but then I had no choice. Now, I do. A gentle touch on my arm startles me and draws my attention. Sebastian gives me an encouraging smile. His hand drops from my arm. Its warm presence and gentleness soothe my worried soul.

"Look who we have here." Mabel's high-pitched teacher voice sounds from the corner of the room. "Little Olive and Ruby."

Mabel comes closer and takes Olive and then Ruby, balancing them both on her hips. They eye each other off before Ruby giggles, and then Olive follows suit. A bit of my worry slips away — only a little, though. "Oh, they're going to get along great, and are you going to help me out with these terrible two?" she asks Rylee, who grins eagerly.

Mabel's eyes flick between mine and Sebastian's. "Run along, kids. We're going to plan a double birthday party for these two." She shuffles a little, causing the girls on her hips to laugh more. "Rylee's going to help me, aren't you?"

"Yay, party time," she cheers.

We say our goodbyes, and Olive doesn't even cry or reach for me. We walk outside the granny flat and into the early morning sunshine. "Wow, not how I expected it to go." I breathe in.

"I know what you mean, but now I feel as though I've lost two limbs."

I laugh and backhand him. "They're right in that door. Do you want to get them back or go do something?"

He shoves his hands in his jean pockets and rocks back on his heels. "Let's go crazy without our kids," he jokes.

"How good are you at horseback riding?" I

cock an eyebrow and try not to laugh as his face sobers up, the grin that was there a minute ago now gone.

Clearing his throat, he says, "I'm not experienced if that's what you're asking."

"Come on. Let's get you in the saddle." I reach out, grip his hand, and pull him along with me. Moments later, I realize I'm still holding it even though he's walking right beside me. I move to let go, but his grip tightens as does the grip around my heart. His hands aren't what I expected of a Formula One racer. I thought they'd be calloused, but his are soft and tender. After another second, he lets go, and we keep walking to the big barn where most of the horses are kept.

When we enter, Hudson and Harley are there at the reception desk. At the same time, they both stand, eyebrows raised, and they both look as though they've just caught me with my hand in the cookie jar. My cheeks heat, but I push that embarrassment aside and move toward them.

"Hey, are there two horses we can borrow for a little while? I'm teaching Sebastian to ride. I think he should learn how hard it is before he puts his daughter on one."

They both chuckle. Hudson runs his hand through his hair while Harley still stares at me, then Sebastian. They glance at each other and then back at Sebastian and me. "Holly and Dolly are free."

"We've got a horse called Dolly now?"

"Yes," they answer in unison.

"Well, okay then. Is she with Holly?" I jerk a thumb over my shoulder. I know where Holly's stall is, but I've never met this Dolly.

"Come on. We'll show you," Hud says. I don't miss his mischievous grin.

What game are these two playing at? They're up to something.

Coming around the corner, I see why. Holly and a horse, I'm guessing is Dolly, are saddled up and ready to go as if they knew I'd come looking for a horse or two. "How did you know?" I ask dryly. Sebastian stares between us, looking slightly confused.

"Mabel gave us a heads up this morning," Harley offers. "They're ready to go."

"What's going on?" Sebastian asks.

"Sebastian, these two clowns are my brothers, Hudson and Harley." I gesture to them. They extend their hands, and Sebastian shakes them. "It seems my sister, Mabel, who has the kids, must have told these two that we might need some horses.

"Oh, well, it's worked out well then. Now let's see if I can even get on one, let alone ride it."

"You're not afraid of a little horse, are you, considering you race at some of the most dangerous speeds?"

He laughs. "That's different."

"No, it's not. It's worse than riding." I turn back to my brothers and roll my eyes at them. I'll be having a silent word with Mabel and these two later. "Are the same tracks open?"

"Yeah," Harley answers, and he and Hudson turn away, fist-bumping each other. I could kill them.

Sebastian stops in front of a tall, chestnut Arabian beauty. "I'm supposed to ride that? She's so tall."

Biting my bottom lip, I grin. "She's the same height as Holly. You'll be fine. These horses have to have some level of patience, especially when working with special needs children. They sense your fear, so pretend you're about to race. Do you get nervous?"

He casts me a sideways glance. "All the time. Every race is different, and you don't know what's around the next corner. Your body is so tense the entire time. It's very challenging."

"Then this should be easy for you." I clap him on the shoulder. "Come on. Take up her lead, and we'll take them to the beginning of the horse trails we have around here."

I step up to Holly. She throws her head in the air and then steps forward and headbutts my chest. "Ow, I get it. You're mad at me." I rub down her neck and then along her nose. She moves her head and then nips at my shirt. "Don't do that, Holly. I'm sorry I was gone so long. Let's go for a ride like old times. How does that sound?"

She neighs a little and starts walking away. I reach and grab her reins and turn to find Sebastian giving me one of his devilish grins I see plastered over the television when he wins a race. This one is slightly different, though—more meaningful in a way. "You ready to go?" I nod in the direction of the open barn door.

"She understands you?"

"Who? Holly?"

He nods.

I rub Holly's nose, and she tugs on the lead, indicating she wants to keep going. "Yeah, she does. They're pretty smart animals once you get to know them. Come on, before she yanks off my arm, and I'll tell you our story."

"Sounds interesting." He keeps turning to check Dolly.

I shake my head and lead the way out.

"Have fun," Harley and Hudson call. I throw them a glare through slitted eyes. Those two are such kids. No wonder Olive has taken to them so easily.

"Where to, fearless leader?" Sebastian jokes as he walks a couple of steps behind but beside me. Other people around the ranch glance in our direction. Someone familiar catches my eye—

Devon. He's walking with Odette, holding her hand, but it's not just them. Parker Kent is with them, along with a woman I'm guessing is his wife, Addison.

"Hey, Deee," Odette squeals and lunges for me. Thankfully, Holly and Dolly are trained not to flinch in situations like this, but I catch a glimpse of Sebastian, who grips his lead a little tighter, his knuckles whitening.

I hug Odette, dropping Holly's reins, knowing the horse won't move. "Hey, Odette. Hey, Devon," I greet him over Odette's shoulder. Parker and Addison watch the exchange between us. Odette finally releases me and does a little twirl in a circle. I love her lively spirit. When I look at her, I don't see her disabilities. I see a vibrant girl whose heart is gold and caring.

"Hello, Dee," Devon says as his head twitches to the side.

"This my sister, and this is Devon's sister, Addy," Odette offers an introduction to Parker and Addison.

"Nice to meet you both. Big fan here, Parker," I say while attempting to keep my cool and not leap at him like a crazy person. I extend my hand to Addison and then Parker.

"Good to meet you. Odette here has just been telling us all about you and little Olive."

"Oh, has she now? She can be quite the chatterbox sometimes." I eye her. She's swaying side to side while chewing at her nails. Instinctively, I reach up and pull her hand away and keep it in mine. "This is Sebastian. We were just heading off for a ride to show Mr. King here around the property."

"We did that yesterday. It was great... such a beautiful piece of land. We really enjoyed the creek and had a quick dip... so refreshing. We come here as often as our schedules allow it to spend time with Devon," Addison says while gently bumping Devon's shoulder. My eyes drop to their locked hands and then shift back up to their faces.

"Yes, the creek is beautiful when it's flowing. How long are you guys planning to stay?" I ask as I pat Holly on the neck.

They turn to each other and shrug. "No real timeframe at the moment. Just enjoying some downtime before the new basketball season starts," Parker says while smiling at Addison.

"I can relate to getting downtime before a big season," Sebastian agrees.

Parker points at Sebastian. "You would, being a driver for Formula One. I enjoyed watching you race. When do you think you'll get back to it?"

Addison backhands him in the stomach as if he's done something wrong.

"Ow, what's that for?" he asks.

Addison's face turns beet red as she opens her mouth to respond when Sebastian jumps in.

"Hopefully, next year, unless they need a fill-in driver for the rest of this season. So it's just a waiting game. Not that I mind. I've got the two girls to take care of."

"That's cool. I look forward to seeing you back behind the wheel, hopefully in the not-too-distant future," Parker says excitedly.

I jump in. "Will you be around for the big bonfire we'll have in a couple of nights?"

"I think so. We aren't rushing off anywhere." Addison smiles as she bumps Parker.

"Great, well, we'll catch up again then. It was lovely to meet you both," I say as we all exchange our goodbyes. Devon and Odette walk on with Parker and Addison. Sebastian and I continue our silent walk, leading the horses until we pass his cabin.

"What's the bonfire?" he asks, breaking the silence.

"We do it every weekend, and we started it before I left. It's where the guests, workers, and clients get to hang out. It's always good to have everyone together in a social setting, not just business, and it's a great atmosphere here. We provide a cookout for everyone. It's good fun. Do you think you'll come?"

"Maybe, if you're going."

Chapter 20

Delilah

MY BREATH WHOOSHES FROM MY lungs as I take in his words. I'm sure he didn't mean them the way they came across. "I'll be there," I attempt to respond casually.

"Cool. I'm sure Rylee will have the time of her life."

"I bet she will, especially when the glow sticks come out, and we roast marshmallows."

"Sounds like fun."

I gently tug Holly to a stop at the beginning of the trail walk. "Well, it's time to climb on. Do you think you'll be all right? And make sure that you put your phone in the saddle pocket as well. I've fallen off a few times and shattered my phone numerous times. So, just a precaution." I slip mine into the pocket and spot him doing the same.

He has a nervous chuckle as he takes in Dolly's size, looking her up and down. "I should be."

"Now, you need to put the rein up over her head and hold it there as you climb on. Your foot needs to go in here." I demonstrate which boot and stirrup to use to hoist up onto the horse. I lift myself and settle into the saddle. It's as if I never left. The most natural thing in the world to me is being on the back of a horse, saddled or bareback. I feel free.

Sebastian does exactly as I showed him and settles himself on the horse's back. He wriggles from side to side to find a more comfortable way to sit. "Well, would you look at me on the back of a horse. I'm not sure I'm ready for Rylee to do this, though."

"I wouldn't use a big horse like these two with her. We have smaller breeds for teaching young kids. Don't worry. I wouldn't put her or you in danger. I trust these animals with my life… well, Holly, anyway, because I trained her." His face pales, and his eyes go wide, then he makes a move to get off. I let out a loud laugh. "I'm kidding. Stay on the horse. My brothers wouldn't keep a horse here if it didn't fit into what we use them for. Kids are around these animals daily. Calm down."

"Not funny. I'm already on edge being on this thing. It's no race car, that's for sure."

"Oh, they have so much power. Maybe you can try cantering through an open field."

He shakes his head furiously. "No thanks. I'll leave that to the professionals. Slow and steady here while I find my feet in this saddle."

"Okay, let's get going. What you want to do is give a little click of the tongue and a gentle nudge in the tummy… nothing too aggressive. With the reins, keep them slack, and when we need to navigate, just a gentle tug whichever way we're going."

Sebastian nods as I give my directions. I click my tongue and give a little nudge to Holly, and she heads down the dirt road. My hips move with her body as she takes the lead, and Sebastian and Dolly follow.

I glance over my shoulder. Sebastian's brow is furrowed, and he's looking down at the horse that moves gracefully behind me. "Don't concentrate too hard, or she might read your thoughts and take off on you," I call.

"Oh, be quiet, you. Stop trying to rile me. I'm not sure how Rylee will do on a horse." His knuckles whiten as he grips the reins. I drop Holly back to walk beside them, our legs bumping against each other as the horses move.

"She'll take to it no problem. I've always found that young kids are scared their first few times and only for a short while until they adjust to the horse, and then they're having so much fun. You've got this, big-time race car driver. It's just a different kind of horsepower." Leaning over, I rub Holly's neck. She snorts her appreciation.

"You can say that again, and I swear, my butt is going to be sore tomorrow."

Throwing my head back, I laugh. "You'll be sore in more places than your butt. You'll figure out muscles that haven't been used in a while."

We get to a fork in the road, and I lead Holly to the left and through an open set of gates. Dolly follows Holly's lead. We ride in peaceful silence. The only sounds are the birds in the trees and field, and some cows mooing in the distance. Hooves clack on the dirt road. It's so peaceful. I suck in a deep breath until my lungs are full, and I can taste the pine scent on my tongue.

"You seem relaxed here. The way you ease into the saddle and let the horse take the lead," Sebastian comments.

I turn to him. His eyes are forward on the road ahead. His body has relaxed a little. "I've not felt this kind of peace in a long time. I left three years ago and only came back a day before you got here," I say, not remembering if I've told him already or not.

Those deep eyes, full of concern, take me in. "It was the guy, wasn't it?"

I nod. "Yeah, I found the wrong guy, and the only good thing to come out of that situation is Olive." A bulldozer of emotions rolls through me.

Hurt.

Loss.

Suffering.

If I were a volcano, I'd have erupted ages ago.

"That's not good. I hope things get better for you. Is that guy still hanging around? Must be hard having a kid together," he asks, and I keep my eyes facing forward, not wanting to see what I'm sure will be pity in his eyes. It's always the same whenever I tell people. Yes, I stayed with a bad man. There were good times, but they were never enough to drown out the bad. Even when he became better for a little while, I was waiting for the penny to drop and him to lash out. I was stupid, but I found it hard to leave once I was in that situation. "Remember when I told you I know what it's like to lose someone?"

"Yes," he replies cautiously.

"Well, he... Eli, his name was, ended his life. So, it's just Olive and m-me now." My voice cracks and I'm unable to stop the trickle of tears that slip down my face.

Sebastian reaches for my hand. It's a little awkward, so I call Holly to a halt and turn to Sebastian. Understanding shines in his eyes, not an ounce of pity there. I have no idea why the heck I'm opening up to him. Why is it so easy for me to do so?

He takes my hand. A tingling I've not felt in a long time works its way up my arm and jabs me right in the heart, electrifying me.

"I'm sorry for your loss. Even if he wasn't a

nice guy, it's not an easy thing to go through. If you don't want to talk about it, we can change the subject." His large, warm hand covers mine, which rests on my thigh, and he gives it a gentle squeeze. A calming sensation washes over me at his tenderness.

"It's okay. I've not spoken about it much with anyone. I only told Harley the same day you arrived. None of my other family members know. I hadn't really spoken to them since the night I had a full blow-out with my father three years ago. They weren't there for Olive's birth or for the medical issues I had after. Sometimes I wonder if it was the stress Eli caused me that brought about my health problems after Olive was born." I pour out the words as though I'm a broken faucet, and it feels great not to have the judgment or pity from my family. Spending time with Sebastian and talking to him is so easy and lightens the load I'm carrying on my shoulders and dragging behind me.

"Your scar?" Those chocolate-like eyes bore into mine.

"Yes, I—" I snap my mouth shut. Do I want to admit this to him? "I had complications after having Olive, and my heart became enlarged and damaged. I am lucky to be alive, but the only problem was that I needed a heart transplant. I was waiting, and Eli wouldn't bring Olive to me, so I'm guessing that's where I ran into you. Not long after that, I got my transplant. Otherwise, I wouldn't be here." Moving my hand from his, I swipe away the dampness on my cheek. "But hey, you don't want to hear my sob story."

"I mean, you probably already know mine since it was blasted all over the news. I'm happy to listen if you've never talked to anyone about it. I'm more than happy to be that person for you." He gifts me a grin that stirs something in my stomach, causing butterflies.

"How about I race you to the creek, and then we can talk?" Without his reply, I give Holly a little kick, and she takes off at a slow gallop. Dolly catches on and quickly follows.

"What the—" Sebastian cries, and I glance back to see him scrambling to stay in his saddle. We aren't going that fast, so he has plenty of time to make his adjustments to stay put. Laughter bubbles from my mouth as a rush of exhilaration is doused over me.

It's been so long.

Too long.

Chapter 21

Sebastian

"YOU PLANNED THAT, DIDN'T YOU?" My nerves rattle around inside me like a heap of loose nuts and bolts on an old truck. She got me good, and that laugh was magic to my ears. If my near-death experience makes her giggle, I'm sure I could stop that by taking her on a hot lap in one of the safety vehicles on the track.

Dolly follows at a good speed. Thank goodness for the little knobby thing on the saddle — it stopped me from toppling from my seat. This isn't the easiest thing I've done. Give me a Formula One car and track any day over a horse.

We come to a little stream about two feet wide. Medium-size greenery and some tall trees are scattered along the bank which borders the blue-green water. This is what I call heaven. I'm so glad I came here. I'll have to bring the girls down and maybe have a picnic.

"This place is beautiful." I sigh. The sun sparkles as it hits the clear water.

Dee slips off the horse gracefully. I attempt to follow her moves, but my foot catches in the stirrup. I jump around on one leg until I manage to get my foot loose and then fall in the dirt. A cloud of dust surrounds me as the dirt settles onto my jeans.

Delilah laughs—she practically cackles. Her arms wrap around her stomach as she drops to her knees, full-on belly-laughing. Getting up, I race toward her and scoop her up. She stops laughing.

"What are you doing?" she cries while still giggling. It's then she realizes, stops, and tries to get out of my arms. I grip her tightly against my chest. Her heat radiates through me, stirring something within me as if shaking the invisible dust and cobwebs from my withered heart and giving it life again—giving me life again. Joy at the connection with another woman. *What would Anna-Beth think?*

"Put me down," she cries again, pulling me back to the present.

"Okay, I'll put you down." Stopping at the creek edge, I bend over and drop her into the shallow water — jeans, boots, and all. She screams and bolts upright, then lunges for me, taking my hand and yanking me toward the water.

Once in the water, she moves closer to the bank and stands in front of me. Before I can stop her, Delilah pushes me in the chest, causing me to stumble backward into the deeper part of the water, and every part of me is drenched — clothes, runners, and all.

Oh, she's going to get it now. She runs away behind the horses, and we do this silly little dance as she avoids me. "I'm going to get you, eventually." I laugh.

"Are you, though? I mean, I could jump on Holly and take off. You haven't seen any of my skills yet." She waggles her eyebrows playfully. The stir of desire comes in hot and fast. I rush her, and after a moment, I get a hold of her arms. Throwing her over my shoulder, I go back to the creek's sandy bank.

"Now you're in for it." I run into the water and drop her from my shoulder. She gets up, her hair wet and sticking all over her face. She wipes it away. I laugh at her swamp-monster look as she wraps her arms around me and tries to pull me down. My hands slide around her.

Everything slows as I take in our position. Her big blue eyes are wide and glittering with happiness. They shift from my eyes to my mouth and back up again. Ever so slowly, so as not to frighten her, I lean into her and bump her nose with mine. Her eyelids flutter closed and then open. Our breaths mingle. Tenderly, I brush my mouth over hers, a featherlight kiss on her strawberry-pink lips, and her body trembles beneath my touch. I tighten my hold on her, pulling her against me. The gentle sound of rushing water is the only sound around us.

Delilah pushes up on her tiptoes. Our mouths crush harder together. Our tongues dance and taste each other. This moment isn't what I was expecting today. But why does it feel so right?

Chapter 22

Delilah

A HUNGER I HAVEN'T FELT in a long time bubbles to the surface, and I want Sebastian's kisses and touches all to myself. Eli had stopped being sweet and gentle almost as soon as we left the ranch. Sebastian ignites a flame that had been extinguished almost three years ago.

The kiss slows, and he pulls away. His hands stay resting on my hips, and I relish his possessiveness.

"I'm sorry," we both say in unison, then chuckle.

"I wasn't expecting anything like that to happen," he says as he reaches up and moves my damp hair from my face, then glides his thumb down my cheek.

"Neither was I," I admit while I internally freak out. I kissed Sebastian-freaking-King. I must be dreaming. "I think you're going to have to pinch me because I'm not sure if this is real. These things don't happen to me. It's like a scene from a Hallmark movie." And now I have a moment to process, freak out. My thoughts turn back to Eli and that hole of emotions I haven't dealt with yet. I'm not sure how to.

Am I a bad person for not mourning him properly? I haven't even read his suicide note. The police read it, and when they could, they gave it back to me. When I moved back to the ranch, I shoved it in the darkest part of my wardrobe. That's not dealing with it—it's hoping it will go away. It's not like I *have* to know what it says.

My palms rest on Sebastian's firm chest. I can't bring myself to look at him. Shame washes over me so fast that it blindsides me.

"I'm sorry. I shouldn't have," I mumble and drop my hands from his chest and make a move to go around him. His grip tightens, and he pulls me back in front of him. He uses one finger and lifts my chin to meet his heated gaze. There's a fire blazing in his eyes.

"You don't need to be sorry. I should be. It's clearly too soon, but I couldn't help myself. It's like there's an invisible rope pulling me toward you, and I don't know how to cut it. I've wanted to hang out with you since the day I arrived."

I scoff and go to look away, but he moves his head to keep in my eyesight.

"Delilah, what's wrong? Come on. Let's sit and talk."

In a daze, I sit in the cool water on the bank of the stream. It's calming. A comfortable silence falls between us as he sits close beside me. "I'm not sure what to say," I tell him. My brain has gone to mush. I'm somewhere in between cloud nine and earth. Perhaps this is a thunderstorm.

"What are you feeling? I mean, I'm pretty happy with what just happened between us. You were so happy, and then when your smile disappeared. I've never been more nervous. Well, except on my wedding day and first Formula One race," he says.

I grin and bump his shoulder with mine. He lifts his arm and wraps it around my shoulders.

"I don't regret that it happened. A part of me wonders if it's real or if I'm dreaming. Like, you're Sebastian King... you would have no interest in a small-town girl like me. I think I'm so far from the person you would normally go for," I say, even though it's only the tip of the iceberg when it comes to my issues right now. There are more issues hidden underneath, and they're always the hardest to work through.

"It's the small-town girl thing that draws me to you, I think. Or it's one of them." He offers me an encouraging grin.

My fingers dance in the stream. I dip them in, lift them, and let the water drip from my fingers.

"Thanks for your encouragement. I think my issues run deeper, though. If I'm being honest, I'm not sure I have fully dealt with the loss of Eli. I know you probably think he doesn't deserve that kind of mourning, and you're probably right. I can't help it. He's only been gone almost six months, and my brain is battling my heart. They're fighting with each other. One tells me to forget about Eli and move forward with my life, and the other is telling me I'm doing the wrong thing by kissing you, but I know that's just conditioning. Eli had control over me. Heck, I still have the letter from him he left, but I've never been able to open it."

Sebastian's arm tightens around me. "It's okay to feel those things. I felt them and still do with Anna-Beth. It's almost been a year since her passing, and even as I kissed you, like you, I had a war within me as well. After lots of therapy when I lost her, I can tell you that it's okay and normal to feel how you do. We loved them. They were our persons for such a long time and hold a piece of our hearts. Even if Eli wasn't a great guy, you still loved him, just like I loved Anna-Beth. What you're feeling is normal."

His words are a comfort and cause tears to well in my eyes. Eli has always been the person of my nightmares. Even when things turned ugly and hurtful, I didn't stop loving him. He'll always hold a piece of me, and it's up to me *not* to allow him to continue to take my happiness from me. He's done that for long enough. "You're right. I never did the therapy thing. I probably should have."

"I'll be your grief therapist. I've clocked a good number of hours in that department. Our circumstances are different, but it all still applies. Eli doesn't own you… remember that. I'm not saying forget about him and move on as fast as you can. Healing and accepting are some of the hardest parts of loss, no matter how we lose our loved ones."

"Gee, you're really good at this." I turn my head to meet his dark eyes. They hold so much hope. I wish mine could hold it too, but it's going to take a bit more time in the healing department before I get there.

He shrugs. "Like I said, I've spent a good lot of hours in the chair talking with a therapist. I'd be happy to help you find someone to talk to."

I shake my head. "No, I don't want to see a therapist. Simply being back home is helping, being back where I belong, where the horses are my therapy. Working with them, talking with them… they don't talk back, and that's just fine with me. I also have Olive. Right now, she's enough to bring anyone to tears with her sleepless nights," I joke.

"Delilah, you need to deal with Eli. Read the letter and then burn it if you want. Give yourself some closure. It's the best thing you could do for yourself."

"How did you deal with the death of Anna-Beth?" I ask in a small voice.

"Well…" he looks off into the distance before meeting my eyes again, ". . . well, I had plenty of therapy," he jokes, a playful grin on his face. I simply shake my head. "Seriously, for me personally, it was knowing that she was living on by helping others live their lives."

My back straightens. His arm falls from my shoulders. "What do you mean?"

"She was an organ donor. So to me, she's still here with us just helping others live." The way he speaks about her is beautiful, and I hope I have someone who speaks about me as he does her in my future.

"That's so wonderful," I gush, but now my interest is piqued. "Have you ever looked up who received something from her?" The pounding in my chest intensifies.

He shakes his head. "I can find out if I want to but haven't felt the need to go down that path."

"Would you want to meet someone? How do you think it would make you feel?" I'm bursting at the seams, wanting to tell him my hypothesis. It's not a good idea, though. I hardly know the man, and it possibly won't go down well if I blindside him.

He shrugs and then reaches into the water for a handful of sand, which he lets fall through his fingers. "I don't know. Wouldn't it be a little weird? I wouldn't know how to think or react. They would have a piece of her. She helped many people, and for that, I'm grateful. Maybe when I feel the time is right, I'll look into it."

I release my breath slowly. He'll be long gone before that happens. He won't be staying here forever, and I'll be left on my own again. I can't fall for him. But the kissing is wonderful. I've missed that connection. It's not something I'll forget any time soon.

Clearing his throat, he says, "Thanks for doing this with me today. Maybe not for the fully-clothed dip, but I'm really enjoying myself. It's exactly what I needed to escape the stress that's been clinging to me lately." He leans over and presses his lips to my cheek, only I wish it was my mouth instead.

Angling my head to face him, I reach up and cup his cheek. "I want you to know I don't regret the kiss. In fact, I wouldn't mind if it happened again sometime."

Chapter 23

Delilah

"THEIR STALL IS READY FOR them with fresh water and some food. What happened to you two?" Harley hollers as Sebastian and I step through the barn door over an hour later, probably looking like drenched rats. Ignoring him, we lead the horses back into their shared stall and unsaddle them. Once I'm finished with Holly, I help Sebastian, his body indecently close to mine. Once Dolly is unsaddled, I hand Sebastian a brush. "Brush her down, and I'll do Holly."

Harley barrels up to the gate. "We ended up in the creek," I finally answer Harley's question. I side-eye Sebastian, and his focus is fully on me while he's aimlessly brushing down Dolly. *Swoon.* There go those heart palpitations he causes.

"More like someone pushed me in," Sebastian says with a wry grin and accusatory tone.

"No, you started it by throwing me in." I shove him in the arm.

"Well, yeah, that was me, wasn't it?"

"It wasn't Holly here, that's for sure." Turning to Harley, I say, "It's his fault."

Harley's grin spreads from ear to ear as he takes in the exchange in front of him, and then it clicks. I see his mischievous eyes ticking with ideas and thoughts on what's going on with Sebastian and me. When he catches me staring, he shrugs and mouths, *"What?"*

Sebastian's full focus seems to be on brushing Dolly down now. I shake my head at my brother and go back to the job at hand.

"It sounds like a good ride. I checked in on Olive and the girls before, and they were all having the time of their lives. It's only them in there today, so Mabel is fully attentive to the girls. Oh, and Dee, I'm Olive's favorite uncle."

I face him, my hand cocked on my hip. "Are you now?"

"Yes, Hudson and I ran a test."

"A test?"

He nods. "We both sat in the corner of the vacation care, and Mabel put Olive on the floor to see who she'd come to, and it took her a moment and a promise of a horse, but her little legs moved in my direction so fast." He stands tall and kind of puffs out his chest. "Oh, and Sebastian, I'm your girls' favorite as well, but I'm not sure if it's because Olive came to me or the horse thing. I think it was because of the horse thing. Rylee screamed with excitement."

That brings laughter from all of us. I shake my head again at Harley, whose arms are crossed over, resting on the gate.

Of course, Harley would want to claim that title and beat Hudson. Those two are super competitive, and it's only become worse as they've gotten older. The big kids.

"Thanks for that," Sebastian says. "I'm in no hurry to buy any horses or ponies because after my experience today, I'm scared for her to get on one." He says it as though it's a joke, and we all have a little chuckle, but I can see he's being serious. His smile is strained, and the worry lines on his forehead crinkle.

"She'll be riding a little horse compared to Dolly." I gently smack her on the behind a few times. "I'll show you after we're done here. Rylee is safe with me."

"That's a hundred percent the truth," Harley throws in his own opinion. "If you want your daughter learning from anyone, it's Dee. We call her the horse whisperer. She's always had a way with these animals, and no one we've had while she's been away has measured up when it comes to the magic she works with these beauties. I can't wait to see how those three in the other barn come along."

I set my brush aside and make my way to the gate. Sebastian follows suit. "Thanks, Harley. Diamond is a tricky one, though. She's going to need the most work of all of them. When is the vet coming? It's been days, and I need them checked to make sure they're all good to go."

"He said tomorrow. He's been busy with the neighboring ranches. It seems to be birthing season for little lambs. I think Dad's going to buy a few." Harley gestures toward Dad's office on the other side of the barn.

"Oh, my goodness, they're going to be so cute, but I'm not getting up to feed them bottles. I'm already a zombie because of my daughter," I say. Harley and Sebastian chuckle while I unhook the gate and exit the stall, Sebastian following close behind. "Come with me, and I'll show you the horse I'll let Rylee ride. Where's Butter?" I ask Harley.

"He's in a therapy session at the moment in the far round pen." He points to the back of the barn. I know exactly where he means—this place hasn't changed much at all. Why would you change something that's working and thriving?

"Come on." I wave an arm to Sebastian. Our clothes are still wet, and as I flick my hair back, drops of water spill to the ground. "I think I'm going to need another shower because of our little dip."

"You and me both. Damp me and the horse scent don't really mesh well together. Well, that's just me thinking out loud. It was still a great time." He steps into line with me as we exit the barn.

Behind the barn is a large open field. Horses and their trainers and clients are busy in quite a few pens. White metal fences outline each separate space. I make my way down the middle of the pens, and in the far back corner, I spot Butter, a stunning chestnut pony. She's got a small build, but she's super gentle. A teenage girl sits on her back with support workers standing on either side of Butter and another holding the reins.

"Hold here," a worker says with a smile and taps the horn. The brown-haired girl with high-tied pigtails tries to speak, but she can't seem to form a sentence—just a series of broken-sounding words. The workers appear to understand what she needs, and one of them takes her hand.

"It's okay. Butter is gentle. She'll keep you safe," she assures the girl. I can see the fear in the guest's eyes. Instinct takes over because I remember seeing Odette in this same situation. The workers are great, but some of these kids need to feel in control, and she's not getting that right now.

I climb over the fence, grab a lead rope from the fence, and approach slowly. "Hey, guys," I say gently, not wanting to startle anyone, especially the girl. "Do you think I can offer some help?"

All three sets of eyes fall on me, puzzled. "I'm Delilah," I say. Recognition shines in the workers' eyes at the mention of my name.

"Sure. Thank you. She's a bit nervous, and any time we get her on the horse, she won't hold on and let us guide her around," the one who was trying to get the girl to hang onto the horn says.

"I understand. I was watching as I walked over." I glance up at the girl. Her pale cheeks are flushed with pink, and her eyes are red with unshed tears. These little souls—they're so beautiful, and it's hard when their bodies won't let them communicate what they want. "Hello, I'm Dee. What's your name?"

The girl's eyes focus on me, and her hand comes up as a finger points to her chest. Following her direction, I notice the badge she wears. Taking a step closer, I read her name tag. "Claire?"

She nods and does a little wiggle in the seat as if trying to get Butter to move.

"Do you want Butter to move?" I ask, and she gives another nod. "Okay, let's try something."

I reach for Butter, giving her a pat down her nose and then along her neck. I glance back at the man holding the reins. "I'd like you to hand the reins to Claire, please."

His brow furrows as he purses his lips.

"It's okay. I know what I'm doing." I attach the lead rope I'd grabbed to Butter's bridle. He nods and works the reins up so Claire can hold them.

Claire moves her hand and makes the sign language move for 'thank you.' I smile. "You're welcome," I sign back. It's been a hot minute since I've used it. Everyone who works here has to know it or learn it because we have a vast range of clients, and we like to accommodate as many people as possible. "Don't pull too tight, or Butter will stop. Hold her gently, okay?" I hope she understands, but she nods again, and then I click my tongue, and Butter moves at the sound, slowly walking.

Claire gives a little squeal of delight, and the smile on her face could light up any dark room.

I say, "Woo," and Butter reacts again by stopping. I look up at Claire. "Wait one minute." I hold up my finger and then turn to the three workers. "Sometimes the clients want to feel in charge. Butter works on sounds as well as being led. I click my tongue to get him walking and say "woo" to get him to stop. You guys are doing amazing."

They all give their thanks. I turn and walk away, unable to wipe the grin from my face. Sebastian stands at the fence, smiling, his eyes bright and only on me, but someone farther back catches my eye as well—Dad. He gives a small half-smile before turning away and going about his business. A surge of happiness pumps through me at finally settling in and helping others. It's what I always wanted to do, and training the horses is my therapy.

"That was impressive." Sebastian nods in Butter and Claire's direction.

Claire is happily riding Butter while being led around. It brings a tear to my eyes. "Butter is a good horse." As I climb back over the fence, Sebastian grabs my hips and assists me down—not that I need it, but it's nice to have the good kind of attention on me. "Thanks. So, will you let me teach Rylee on Butter? Look at Claire's face… imagine it's Rylee's. You would be dad of the year."

He chuckles. "How did you know what to do then?" He points out to Claire and Butter.

I shrug. "Odette," I state simply. "She was very much the same. These support workers are doing a great job, but sometimes they forget to look at the bigger picture and think about the person they're working with. Everyone's different. Odette would get so upset, in tears and screaming because she didn't want to be led again… she wanted to hold the reins, and that little gesture gave them a sense of control since they can't control other parts of their bodies, minds, and everyday lives. Being on a horse can calm them. Some are happy to be led around, no problem. Claire simply wanted to be in charge, and the way I trained these horses, I trained them to respond to sounds. Like a click of the tongue is go, and 'woo' is stop. All horses should have it, but again, I've been gone for three years, so I'm not sure who the newer horses were trained by."

Without a word, Sebastian wraps me up in his arms, holding me tightly for a moment. "Thank you for showing me a different side of the world. I've been kept in the dark about most disabilities and special needs kids. They really are special in every kind of way. I'd love to find a way for some kids to come to a Formula One race and come in the paddock to meet some racers and fellow engineers and mechanics. Just so many people. I want to see that smile you put on Claire's face on a heap of other kids. Heck, I'd be happy to start a foundation or something to help those who may need it and to give them something special." He says all this into my neck, and my arms tighten around him. He lifts me off the ground and spins in a circle.

"That would be an amazing opportunity for these kids, but not only kids... adults as well. Maybe it's something to look into for a time in the future."

He releases me but runs his hands down my arms and links our fingers together. My chest tightens with anticipation. His touch is powerful—I've had one little bit, and I keep going back for more. "I'll see. I hope you realize I'll be looking into this."

"That's good. I have every faith you can achieve anything you put your mind to," I say.

He moves nearer, his heated stare on my mouth. The world around us fizzles away as he gets closer and closer. My pounding heart sounds in my ears. Sebastian leans in, and not for the first time today, his mouth is on mine.

Chapter 24

Sebastian

SHE TASTES LIKE SWEET CANDY and is completely addictive. Her mouth molds to mine, and I want to kiss her daily. It's been so long since I had an intimate connection with anyone, and my body comes alive with desire and the want to claim her.

Our breaths mingle, and within a moment, she pulls back. "Maybe we should slow down a little. Don't get me wrong, you're amazing. It's just I worry we don't know each other well enough." Her hands rest on my chest, and mine still on her hips.

"If that's what you want, I'm okay with that. I don't want you to feel uncomfortable at all." I want her to feel as though she can come to me for anything, and I'd happily be her savior. This pull between us is getting tighter. Why?

Delilah takes a step back, out of my grip. Her mouth is pink and well-kissed, her breaths not settled yet. "Let's just see what happens. You possibly won't be here for much longer, and you have a busy life somewhere else. You'll also be traveling for your work again soon."

I scoff. "Maybe, if my manager can find me a seat to race in. My team has handed my seat to someone else because I'd taken time to grieve my wife and care for my girls. Hopefully, next year I'll be back at it."

She smiles, but it doesn't reach her eyes. "I know. You're a big superstar racer. You've got to get back to it, and that's totally okay."

Why do I feel as though she's pulling back from me?

"Do you still want to spend time with me while I'm here?"

She shrugs, and her eyes blink furiously. "I'd like to. It's fun spending time with you and having someone understand what I'm going through. Not many people do. My family understands loss since we lost our mom, but I have to tell them about Eli tonight. Who knows how Dad will react, or any of them, for that matter?"

Reaching out, I take her hand. "If you need me, you know where I am."

"Thanks," she says and squeezes my hand.

"Now, I think I'm going to have a shower before I get chafed in places I don't want." She laughs.

I shake my head. "Same. What are you doing after that?"

"Well, I've got to go down and check on the horses and work with them for a few more hours. I'll stop in and check on Olive as well."

"Oh, I wouldn't step foot in there because the moment you do, they'll want you and won't let you leave. Trust me, I did that the first few times when I took the girls to vacation care back home, and I learned some big lessons those days. Maybe just message your sister to see how things are going," I offer.

We start walking back past the fenced pens toward the barn. "Okay, I'll do that. Which reminds me, we need to get our phones from the saddles."

After we collect them, we go our separate ways — her toward the homestead and me back to my cabin. Thoughts of Delilah invade my mind — her beautiful blonde hair, wet and stuck all over her face. I laugh at the memory. Her soft touch and skin I want to trace my fingers across so much, and her bright blue eyes that pierce me right through the chest.

Everything about her is breathtaking, and I want to spend more time with her. She's right, I'll be leaving. And where will that leave us? I'm not sure I can walk away from her, though. That sounds so crazy. Maybe it's the fact we have some understanding of each other about our deceased loves. Although this Eli guy—I wish I could've read between the lines a year ago when I first met Delilah.

Could I have helped her out of the situation she was in? Probably not—not in the state I was in after losing Anna-Beth. I could hardly handle the girls or my own turmoil at the time. Perhaps it's no coincidence that we've been brought together now to possibly help each other, and not for any other reason, at a time when we're both finally ready to give and receive it.

It's crazy how the world works. I walk past the small barn where I know she'll be working in a little while. My chest surges with excitement at the thought of seeing her again. Will she want me to come and talk to her? I'd be interested in seeing how she does what she does with the horses. It amazed me seeing her work with Butter and Claire. I need to make a few phone calls and start a program or something for special needs kids in Formula One. They all have different passions, and I'd love to show support for them. Something needs to change.

My phone sounds off with a message. I take a look and can't help my grin.

> **Delilah:** *Thanks for a fun morning. It was something I desperately needed but didn't realize it.*

Delilah has had it rough by the sounds of it, and if Eli were still alive, she probably wouldn't be here—back in her home—with her family. It sounds like he took her freedom from her, and that breaks my heart. Now, it seems like she's trying to find her feet again, and I'm all for helping her do that.

I type a quick reply.

> **Sebastian:** It's my pleasure. I enjoy spending time with you. It's been a while since I took care of me and being here at the ranch and meeting you has made a world of difference.

> **Delilah:** I know what you mean. It's been Olive and me for the last six months, and before that, I didn't do anything for myself. I hardly left the house.

> **Sebastian:** Why didn't you go out? Didn't you have friends or a job?

> **Delilah:** No and no. Eli made sure of that. Plus, I hated leaving the house in case I ran into someone, and I sometimes had visible bruises. I couldn't do the judgment. I've never told anyone what I've told you about Eli. Like I said, he wasn't a great guy.

> **Sebastian:** I'm sorry you went through all of that. If I could take some of that pain away from you, I would, gladly. No one should feel as you did. I'm glad you're comfortable talking with me. I'm all ears and ready to listen. Anytime.

> **Delilah:** Thanks. Now I need to figure out a way to get these wet jeans off.

Sebastian: If you need help, give me a call. LOL!

Delilah: I'm sure I can manage.

She puts a winking emoji at the end of her message, and I laugh. I trudge up the few steps and unlock my cabin. It's so weird to be alone and in an empty home. The girls are a big piece of my days now, and I'm usually having a shower when I know they're asleep at night.

Stripping down and after having to wriggle my way out of my jeans, I step into the steaming-hot water. Knowing Delilah is doing the same shoots want through me. What if I could see her doing that at the end of the day? What if I could see her perfect body every day?

I mentally slap myself.

Time to get my head out of the clouds.

I'll be leaving soon.

Chapter 25

Delilah

TYING MY HAIR IN A messy bun, I make my way out of my room and go to head down to the kitchen and get some lunch before going to the horses. My feet stop in front of the library door. The desire to clear this room out is overpowering, but my heart isn't ready for it. After hearing how Dad looks at this room, it frightens me to open the door again. His theory isn't wrong, but I want Olive to love spending time with me in this room as much as I loved spending time in there with Mom.

Turning away, I continue downstairs and along the hall to the kitchen, where Sybil, Odette, and Devon are sitting at the table with a plate full of sandwiches in the middle of them.

"Hey, Dee," Odette greets me in her higher-than-normal people voice.

"Hey, Odette. What's for lunch?" I ask.

"Sandwiches. Do you want one? We've made heaps," Sybil answers. I grab a bottle of water from the refrigerator and take a seat with them while snatching up half a peanut butter and jelly sandwich.

I take a bite and groan. "I haven't had one of these in such a long time. I know that sounds crazy, but it's true. And this tastes so good."

"We have it all the time," Odette offers as she picks up another half.

"That sounds yummy. What have you guys been up to today?"

"Not as much as you, apparently," Sybil mutters under her breath with a cheeky grin.

"What? Who said what?" I stab a finger in her direction across the table. Devon and Odette seem oblivious to the conversation, and they continue to chat about the horses and discuss some suggestions about the ranch moving forward.

"Let's just say that Harley and Hudson filled me in on what you got up to this morning." Sybil winks, and I inwardly cringe.

"Who else have they told? I don't want people to think anything because we're nothing more than friends. Surprisingly, we have quite a bit in common."

Her eyebrows shoot skywards. "Really? How so?"

"I'm not telling you right now. I'll share all in due time."

"You've always been the queen of keeping secrets." Sybil groans.

I shrug. "What can I say? I'm a pro now."

"Yes, you are," she says monotone as she takes another bite of food.

We finish our lunch, and I thank them, then head out to the horses. I've only got a little bit of time before I need to get Olive and begin our little afternoon routine before I put her down for bed. I can't help but wonder if Sebastian will be out and about. I'm so worried about whatever this is we have going on. He's a great kisser, so tender, yet so hungry for more. I get my phone from my back pocket and shoot off a message to Isla. She'll know what to do.

> **Delilah:** I need help. Sebastian and I kissed today... twice. I have no idea how to handle this. He's so nice and everything I'm not used to. Eli was the complete opposite. HELP!

I'm not expecting a quick reply, but her fingers must move like The Flash.

> **Isla:** YOU KISSED HIM? Wow.

> **Delilah:** Yes, and now I don't know what to do. I should know—I'm old enough to know these things, but my head is all over the place. I feel guilty over Eli and how quickly things have moved with Sebastian. I have told him we need to keep moving slowly, and he was fine with it.

Isla: *I'm sitting here with my mouth hanging open, staring at my screen. I can't believe you kissed him—twice. I think we need to celebrate, but I can tell you're freaking out so we can do that later. Talk to me.*

Delilah: *It's only been a short while since I buried Eli. Is kissing another person and having some feelings for them the wrong thing? And the fact that I've known this person hardly two weeks. It's all too much for my messed-up head at the moment.*

Isla: *Tell me what and how this happened.*

I have to work with these horses for a bit—especially Diamond. Typing and walking is the easiest thing. I fill her in on the horse ride, what happened with Claire and after Claire. My heart hammers even as I go back to those moments in my mind. My stomach swirls with excitement.

I enter the barn to the sound of horses moving around in their stalls and the soft crunch of them chewing hay. "Hey, pretties. Are we ready to get to work?" I go to Diamond's gate first. Her head comes up, her ears prick and turn in my direction. "Hey, girl. Ready to try again? You're such a good girl." After unlatching her gate, I step in.

Diamond moves a little. I stand just inside the gate, closing it behind me. Slowly, I move closer. "You're a beautiful girl," I say softly. She doesn't move or turn away from me—this time, she lets me pat her nose. A wide grin pulls across my face. After not training a horse for so long, this feeling of success makes tears fill my eyes. I run my hand down her neck and give her some scratches. She presses into my hand as if seeking the attention. "I know how you feel, pretty girl. Don't worry. I'll look after you."

An hour later, I've done a little work with each of them, and now I'm absolutely wrecked. My eyelids are heavy and want to close. The sun starts to dip as I make my way up to collect Olive.

When I get to the cabin, the lights are off, and no one's there. My stomach drops. Did I lose track of time? Olive must be wondering where I am. I run up to the house and hear voices floating down the hallway from the kitchen. I go to head in that direction, but I pause when I see the man sitting in the recliner in the living room.

"Dad? What are you doing?"

His head comes up from the book in his lap. I step closer and notice it's a picture album. "Nothing," he says gruffly and snaps it shut. He rises from his seat and walks to the kitchen.

A stab of unease washes over me. Will he ever move on from the past? I don't know what I can do to try to make things right.

"Come on, everyone. Dinner's ready," Tally calls. It's then I hear Olive squeal, and my unease washes away but only briefly.

I scan the room as I enter and spot my little ray

of sunshine fitting right in with the family. Harley's making stupid faces and causing her to giggle, and then everyone in the room laughs. Tally pops a plate of chopped-up food in front of her. She reaches for it, her little hand filled in seconds, and shoves it in her open mouth. Anyone would think she hadn't eaten today.

"Hello, baby girl." I rush to her and smother her in kisses. She beams up at me. Her blue eyes shine with happiness. I hope she lets me sleep through the night tonight. "How was she today, Mabel?"

"She was an angel. She and Sebastian's girls got along great and kept each other entertained. She only got upset when he came and got the girls. So I closed up and came back here where she got entertained by the family clown here." She jerks a thumb at Harley, sitting beside Olive in her highchair.

I can't help but laugh. He really is the family clown and can be sensitive when the occasion calls for it. "Of course. He told me he was her favorite." This causes an uproar between Hudson and Harley.

"No way. I was duped. I want a rematch," Hudson calls from his spot down the table. Odette claps her excitement. Dad silently takes his seat at the head of the table, and I can't sit beside my daughter as she's between Mabel and Harley on the corner. I take a seat beside Harley.

Nerves take over as I realize what I'm about to do—tell my family what happened with Eli and about my health problems. They have every right to know, and I don't want to keep it from them anymore.

"I'm wondering if I could have a moment of all your time," I call, and the table falls silent apart from the clink of forks and knives hitting the glass plates. My eyes land on Harley, who gives me an encouraging smile and goes back to handing Olive bits of her food. He has my back.

"Sure, why not fill us in on what's going on with you and Sebastian. Have you just come home to find another man and run away again? Where's Eli? Can we expect him to turn up, and you just leave again?" Dad's comments slam me right in the heart, and I'm lost for words. How could my father be so harsh? He should be on my side. I thought we were getting somewhere. I guess I was wrong. "I saw you kissing him down at Butter's session this afternoon."

Everyone gasps. My mouth hangs open.

Shutting my mouth, I swallow the lump in my throat and attempt to blink away my tears. He doesn't have the right to treat me this way. It's as if we've gone back in time to the night the fight happened about me being with Eli.

Harley rises from his spot, his face red and a fire in his eyes. "You can't talk to her like that anymore, Dad. She's not a child, and you don't even know the full story." He growls in Dad's direction. All eyes turn to me, and I want to crawl away and hide.

"What's he talking about?" Mabel asks as she moves up beside me. Dad's suddenly mute.

Mabel gently touches my arm, snapping me out of my state of shock. Clearing my throat, I turn to my father. His dark eyes are zoned in on me, and there's a grim look on his face. I hope he eats his words after I tell them my story. "Dad, Eli won't be coming because he died six months ago…"

The room fills with gasps. Mabel's is the loudest as she stands behind me. My glare bores into my father's eyes. His face is stone—he doesn't say anything, so I continue before the questions start pouring in. "He committed suicide. He wasn't the man I thought he was, and I lived with years of abuse because of him. I also had my own health problems. I almost died after I had Olive, but she's what kept me here. She needed me, and I couldn't let her be raised by Eli on her own. Who knows what kind of upbringing she'd have experienced?" I pause, taking some deep breaths in an attempt to control my shaking voice.

"Oh, Dee," Mabel cries beside me. She reaches for me, but I pull back.

"Don't, please. I don't want your sympathy or pity. I'm dealing with it all." The room is silent apart from Olive, who's oblivious to what's happening as Harley keeps her entertained with food.

"Did you know?" Tally asks him accusingly.

His mouth opens to respond, but I jump in. "Yes, he did. I've heard the whispers from you all. I'm back here because I need to heal and not be judged or made to feel like I'm only here to sink my claws into another male staying on the farm. If you knew anything about Sebastian, you'd know he lost his wife about a year ago, and we met in the hospital. I don't remember that, though, because I was in a bad way and had a heart transplant. So yeah, things haven't been great." My tears flow freely. I stab a finger in my father's direction. "You don't have the right to speak to me how you did just now. No father should treat his child how you've treated me."

"Delilah—"

"No, you don't get to speak, not now," I say before he can continue. "You have nothing I want to hear. Not even an apology." I stalk around the table, pull Olive from her highchair, and take off back down the hallway and out the door.

Chapter 26

Sebastian

"DADDY, WILL I GET TO ride the pony soon?" Rylee lays in her bed, her radiant eyes gleaming up at me as she pleads.

I swipe some brown hair from her chubby cheek and give her a kiss on it. "Maybe. I'll have to see what Delilah is doing, and we can arrange something. How does that sound?"

"Sounds good."

"You better get some sleep. You'll need your strong muscles to ride a pony tomorrow. It's not easy. I rode one today and almost fell off." I laugh but deep down, that moment still makes my stomach drop.

She smiles. "But you still got back on, didn't you?"

"I did, and that's the main thing. Sometimes things are hard, but we always have to keep trying to succeed at them." I smile down at her as I sit on the edge of her bed. We're having one of our daddy-daughter moments—the little chats we like to have before bed. She talks to me about her day and if something is bothering her or makes her feel so happy. Anna-Beth would do this with her, and their bond was strong, and I kept the habit going because Rylee needs to know that I've got her, no matter what.

"Will you drive in the fast car again, Daddy?" Her soft voice is full of questions.

I shrug. "I don't know. I want to. Hopefully, next year."

"I hope you can, Daddy. It made you happy, but it also made you mad."

This makes me chuckle. "Yes, it can make me angry, but it only means I'm passionate about something I love. Now, little princess, I think it's time for sleep. We'll go for a walk to the creek tomorrow, and you girls can have a play-around down there. How does that sound?"

"Fun. I can't wait," she cries. I kiss her and tuck her under the blanket.

Out in the tiny living area, I collect my phone from the kitchen counter, where I left it plugged in and charging. I unlock it and call Mom. She'll be wondering why I haven't called these last couple of days.

It rings twice before she answers. "Hey, Sebastian. How are you? How are my girls?"

I grab a beer from the refrigerator and collapse into the couch with a sigh. "Hey, Mom. I'm good, and the girls are having a great time. I thought I'd better call you before you show up here."

"I almost did but thought against it and that I'd give you another day. Tell me what's been going on." She loves details when it comes to her kids.

I take a mouthful of my drink. "Been spending time with the girls, who are having such a fun time. Rylee wants to learn how to ride a horse, and her little heart is set on it."

"Oh, that's exciting for her, and I bet scary for you." Mom gives a nervous laugh.

"I was scared until I saw the horse Delilah planned to put her on. It's such a smart horse as are all of them here. They've all been trained in a specific way, so I'm not too worried anymore." I take another pull of my beer. How much should I tell Mom about Delilah?

"That all sounds wonderful. And tell me about this woman. Has anything more happened? How do you feel toward her?" There it is—her prying voice. She doesn't think she has one, but she does. She sounds a little sly and then attempts to cover it with the littlest of laughs.

"She's doing well. We went horseback riding together today. She told me a fair bit about herself. It's pretty scary how much we're alike."

"How so?" Mom asks as I get up from my spot to raid the pantry and see what snacks I have. Might need to go to the shops at some stage to pick up a few things, especially diapers, since I'm almost out.

"Well, she'd told me she lost someone close to her. It was her husband, but he'd committed suicide."

She gasps. "That's horrible. That poor girl."

"Yeah, she's had it pretty hard by the sounds of it. Her husband wasn't a great man… abusive, she told me. It seems she's trying to find herself again in a way. I get where she's at, though. It took a while for me to find all the pieces and not be stuck together by sticky tape. I had to find the super-glue to keep it together."

"It's not easy, losing someone to suicide… just the thought breaks my heart. I mean, I almost die every time I see you on the racetrack. I've finally gotten my heart in a good place, and you want to go race again." Her voice is stern, but I know she wouldn't expect to see me anywhere else apart from being behind the wheel of a race car.

I laugh. "It's okay, Mom. I haven't heard anything back from them yet, so rest easy for now."

"I will. But enough about you, tell me more about her. Is this the first time you met?"

"No. I helped her in the hospital the day I lost Anna-Beth. She was in there for a heart transplant."

Silence.

Did I lose her?

"Mom?"

She clears her throat. "Honey, have you thought... possibly that she's the recipient of Anna-Beth's heart. If she was in a bad way and moved to the top of the transplant list, it's possible she received it since she was also in the same hospital."

My heart thunders at the possibility. Surely not. Is that why I'm drawn to her? Because her heart is my wife's? "I hadn't thought about it. She did ask the other day if I'd looked into who received an organ from Anna-Beth. Do you think it's possible?"

"Anything is possible, but the question is, what are you going to do with that information if it comes back that she's the recipient? Do you think she's put the timeline together, which is why she asked what she did?"

Mom has all these questions, and I have no answers. Things with Delilah are moving beautifully, and she makes me happy. It's been so long since I've been willing to let the possibility of love into my heart again. "I don't know, Mom. Do you think I should find out if it's true?"

"I don't know... that's your choice. I can't have a say here. You need to think about the possibility that she has it, and if she does, will that change your relationship or friendship... whatever you two have? It's not easy being in your position. We both know Anna-Beth had a heart of gold, and this girl sounds like she's trudged through a swamp of misery, and maybe it was Anna-Beth's heart that led her back to her home, where you eventually ended up. Things happen for a reason."

"Maybe. I'll think on it. It's a lot to take in right now." Now it will be the only thing I think about whenever I see her. The only way to move past this would be to find out the truth and put my mind at ease. "Do you think it would be hard to find out if she got it?"

"I'm not sure, honey. There's a way to look it up, isn't there? But it might take a little bit of time."

"Time is what I seem to have on my hands lately since I haven't heard anything from Luke about a spot for next year. What if I don't get to race again?"

"Sebastian King," she says firmly. "Don't you dare think like that. You'll get a seat next year, even if it's not with the same team. You're a fantastic racer, and you've kept yourself fit and race-ready. You don't pay that personal trainer for nothing. You pay him to keep you at your best, so when you get that chance again, you can slip right back in and kick some butt."

Hearing my mother use the term 'butt' causes me to laugh. "That's not something I usually hear coming from your mouth."

"Well, it was called for. Don't give up on your dreams. You're still the same talented person you were when you left the racing scene. Your turn will come again. I have no doubt."

I go to answer when there's a thunderous knock at the door. My heart stops, and I glance in the direction of the girls' shared room. "Who would be here now?" I mutter.

"What's wrong?"

"Someone's at my door. Hold on." I keep her on the line and go to answer it. Pulling it open, I say, "Mom, I have to go. I'll call you tomorrow." I don't give her a chance to say goodbye when I hang up.

Standing at my door, Delilah clutches Olive, who's got fists full of food. It's like a kick in the stomach, seeing her this way. Her cheeks are flushed and damp with tears. "I'm sorry. I didn't know where else to go." She sobs, and without a word, I pull Delilah against my chest. Delilah's cries tear at my composure. Swallowing the lump forming in my throat, I say, "Come in."

I lead her inside, keeping my arm tightly around her and Olive.

What has happened? I want to hurt the person who has caused her this much pain and anguish.

Chapter 27

Delilah

NOT KNOWING WHERE ELSE TO go, since I didn't have much choice apart from a barn, my car, or driving all the way into town to Isla's place, and none of those options were good enough for Olive, so Sebastian's it was. I never intended to absolutely lose my mind in front of him. I wasn't planning to get upset when I told my family, but my father ruined that, making me feel so little once again. Poor Sebastian. Poor Olive—she didn't even get a chance to eat her dinner or have a bath. This day started good, yet it has turned into a nightmare.

"I'm so sorry," I cry out between hiccups. I must sound like a broken record with all the apologies spilling from my unfiltered mouth. I hug Olive to my chest, wanting her comfort and knowing she will always be there for me, but I also hate this for her. I hate being broken. No one wants someone as broken as me.

I thought I was finding my feet again, and now the ground is crumbling away from beneath me. Or maybe I'm just being dramatic again—that's what Dad would say. I'm sure of it.

"What's wrong, Delilah?" Sebastian guides me to the couch. Once he settles me, he holds his hands out for Olive, and surprisingly, she goes willingly. When she's gone from my grasp, I feel bare. My knees come up to my chest, my arms securing themselves around them. I drop my head down and silently cry.

"She hasn't eaten dinner yet or been bathed. I'm so sorry. My… my father…" I hiccup, not even able to finish the sentence.

"It's okay. I've got something she can have."

I can't look up. I've stormed in here like a bending, winding tornado. Hopefully, I don't leave destruction in my wake.

My father—how could he say those things? Sure, he didn't know Eli's story or mine. Maybe I should've been open right from the beginning, and he'd have understood me better. I didn't come home to find myself a new guy, I came home to heal. To feel a part of something again. At one time in my life, my family was everything. We're a large group, and sometimes we get up in each other's business and drive each other nuts, but we usually work through our problems. It's rare that they get swept under the rug until our next big blow-up.

The vibration in my pocket startles me. I pull out my phone and toss it on the coffee table, then lie down, hiding my face in my hands. I never knew that I'd experience this kind of raw pain again. It's as though my stitches have burst open, and I'm exposed. I won't lie here exposed again— never. I'm not the weak-minded girl I was these past three years. I hiccup one last time and take some deep breaths, pulling myself together.

Olive coos in the background. Sebastian is talking gently to her, and it soothes me at the same time as it seems to soothe her. "Hey, pretty girl. Let's get you fed and have a bath. I even have clothes that will fit you. You look so much like your mama, even down to your cheeky little grin."

She squeals with happiness, and her hands clap on the highchair tray, those little thuds filling the room.

My breathing calms as Sebastian talks, and Olive rambles back. Mama, baba, and everything else that she says brings me so much joy. My phone vibrates, and I ignore it again. I don't want to talk to or see any of my family members.

"Delilah." Sebastian gently touches my shoulder. Pulling my hands away from my face,

I glance up at him. Confusion, uncertainty, and worry fill his eyes. His brow is furrowed. Reaching down, he swipes hair from my face. "What's happened? Do you want anything?"

Slowly, I sit up, my body stiff for some reason. It's as though I've been in one position for ages, and my joints are tight and ache with each movement. "I told my family about Eli and my transplant tonight. My father saw us kiss at Butter's pen, and he basically made me feel as though I only came home to find myself another man and move on. That's not why I came back, and I don't want you to think I'm doing that with you."

He takes my hand and grips it tightly. "I don't think that, and I'm sorry tonight wasn't good for you. You can stay as long as you like, and we can put you and Olive in my bed, and I'll take the couch if you want?"

My stomach forms knots. Shaking my head, I say, "Thank you, but no. I'll go home, but I needed some time away from everyone up there." I nod in the direction of the homestead. I take a deep breath and slowly release it, the tension and sadness from earlier being erased.

"I understand. Stay as long as you like. I'm here for you." He pulls me into his arms in an awkward sitting hug. No matter how weird it is, it's still one of the best hugs I've ever had.

"Thank you so much. Again, I'm really sorry

about this." I glance over his shoulder to Olive, who's happily putting food in her mouth and slapping the highchair table.

He adjusts his shoulder, and his head comes up. He takes my cheeks in his warm hands. "If you want to leave, I'll help you. If you want to stay, I will be here for you. I'm not going anywhere. I think you've already been through enough sad and bad things… we both have. While I'll never forget Anna-Beth, being with you has lit the spark within me, and I want to be able to care for someone again the way I cared for her." Leaning in, he presses his mouth to mine, the night's dirtiness washing away. As quickly as he's there, he's gone again, and I'm left wanting more.

Why do I have this overwhelming sensation to tell him that I like him? I'm drawn to him. I have been from the moment I met him. This is the stupidest time to tell him how I feel, so why is there a pounding in my chest? Butterflies in my stomach move in massive groups, and the urge to speak those words is so powerful it might knock me out of my chair. He has that power over me. It's not the same as the power Eli had—his was about control and order. He bullied me with a do-as-I-say type of dictatorship. I won't ever be a person who accepts that in a partner again. Tonight, I was weak, but tomorrow, not anymore. They now know the truth, and that's all that matters. The rest is history. I need to make my feelings known. No more secrets starting right now.

"I have a confession, though, and I know this isn't the best timing." I sniffle, the tightness in my chest intensifying. "You're a great guy, and I find myself liking you more and more. I feel stupid saying this right now, but, hey, when is it ever a good time to confess these types of things?" I puff out a breath and quickly refill my lungs, remembering to keep breathing in and out.

His smile widens, his white teeth shining, his eyes alive. "Wow, you seem to have taken the words right out of my mouth." He pauses. "I'm not sure where that leaves us, though. I won't be staying long."

His last sentence shatters any hope I had of seeing him in the future. His job and his girls will always come first. "I know," I reply, my voice low. "Perhaps coming here was a bad idea. I should go and sort out my mess. I've settled down now, and I have you to thank for it."

He kisses me again, this time with a slow, deep purpose. Our mouths move as one, and a swell of desire rushes through me. He's tender with his kisses and my heart. If I were to ever fall in love again, I'd want it to be with someone like him. He knows how to treat me, to care for me, and he's discovered how in such a short time. He has captured my heart, body, and soul.

Pulling back, he says, "Wow, you take my breath away."

I chuckle.

With one last brush of our lips, he gets up. "Let's finish feeding her, and we'll see what happens."

When he turns his back, there's a light knock at the front door, and my heart takes off. It has to be someone from my family.

Sebastian's gaze meets my worried one. Without hesitation, he puts on a stone-cold expression and goes to answer the door.

Harley's familiar voice comes from the doorway. "Sorry to bother you, man. Is she here? Tell her it's Harley."

Sebastian glances over his shoulder, a question in his eyes. I nod. He moves aside and lets Harley in.

Harley's soft gaze lands on me. He shakes his head and rushes to my side. "I'm sorry about what happened up there tonight. I should've done more."

Sebastian walks behind the couch and back to Olive in the little kitchen. He obviously knows this is private, but we can't have too much secrecy since it's only a small cabin. I release a puff of air. "No, it's okay. Trust Dad to blow it way out of proportion. What happened after I left?"

Harley gives a low whistle. "Girl, you started World War III up there between the siblings. Dad didn't say much, if anything after you left, but I've never seen him look so pale. I don't think he was expecting you to say what you did. That was like taking a sledgehammer to a wall, and it all just tumbled down over everyone. I'm impressed."

I wipe my hand down my face. "It wasn't my finest moment, but I couldn't have Dad speak to me like he did last time. I'm not a child, and he can't treat me like a teenager like he did when I was with E-Eli." My voice cracks, but I clear it and swallow away the thick emotion in my throat.

Harley pulls me in for a hug. His warmth and calmness envelop me. I have such caring brothers. Harley and I have always had each other's backs, except that one time when he sided with Dad, and I know now he clearly regrets it.

"Tomorrow, you and I are going for a horseback ride out far into the fields. It'll keep you away from Dad for a while, and when you're ready, you can talk to him," Harley says.

"Thanks, Harley. It sounds fun. I'll see how I'm feeling in the morning."

"Mabel and Sybil have offered to take Olive again."

"That's nice, but I'm not sure I want to be apart from her all day again tomorrow."

Harley squeezes my shoulder. "Okay. Well, the offer is there, especially if you want an escape."

"You forget, I have one. I have the horses to

work with. I also want to do the library, and I plan to do some riding lessons with Sebastian's daughter, Rylee." I point in Sebastian's direction.

Sebastian grins. "She was actually asking me about it tonight when I put her in bed."

"It's settled then. I'll spend some time with her in the morning, and then maybe in the afternoon after I've had some time with Olive, we can go for a ride."

"Sounds good to me. Do you want me to take Olive and get Mabel to put her down?" Harley asks.

I shake my head. "No, it's okay. I'll head back up shortly. I've invaded Sebastian's space and cried on his shoulder. I think I've scared him enough." I throw a sideways glance in his direction, gifting him a sugary smile.

"You haven't scared me," he says, and he pulls Olive from the highchair, now fully fed.

Harley nods. "I'll head off then, and I'll see you tomorrow. I wanted to check on you, and I'll report back to the girls and Hudson because they've all been trying to call you. I was the only one game enough to come down here and talk to you."

I wave my hands in the air. "Oh, such a big, brave boy."

We laugh, and it feels great. My lapse earlier was a moment of weakness, and it's okay to have those moments, but I won't let them consume me like they once did.

Sebastian and I say goodbye to Harley, and we're left in silence apart from the garble talk from Olive. I take Olive from his arms. "Thanks for tonight and sorry about falling apart, and thanks for taking care of her." I wiggle Olive in my arms. She giggles.

I step into Sebastian, press my lips to his, and step back.

"Did you want to give Olive a quick bath while you're here? I can go run it for her. I have everything you'd need here for her. She can borrow Ruby's pajamas," he says. It's almost as if he's trying to get me to stay longer.

I chew my lip, thinking over his question. I don't particularly want to deal with my family, and if I go back while they're all awake, I'll have to talk to them. "Sure, I'd love nothing more than to hang with you because I don't want to deal with the mess I left up there." I shrug and try to keep it casual, although internally, I'm high-fiving myself. Sebastian King wants to spend time with me. We've just admitted to having some kind of feelings for each other, and that's crazy to me, but how can I deny my heart at a chance of happiness? That seems to be the thing pulling me toward him—the swell of euphoria he causes within me is completely different from how I felt with Eli. What I had with Eli was puppy love, which turned nasty the moment we left the farm. Sebastian isn't like that. "Lead the way."

He turns, and I follow him to a little bathroom that has a single basin, shower, and bath in one. He pulls the shower curtain to the side and sets about turning on the faucets and making sure the water is at the right temperature. When it is, he pumps some baby wash into the water and swirls it around. This brings a smile to my face. He's such a great dad and overall person. Any girl would be lucky to have him.

No more words need to be exchanged—no more thank yous or sorrys. There's something between us, and it's something we both don't need to discuss—an unspoken bond and pull. It excites me and gives me hope for a bright and happy future.

Chapter 28

Delilah

OLIVE'S HAPPY CHATTER STIRS ME awake, and I peek a glance at the window where there's some soft light. It seems she's finally caught the meaning of 'a good night's sleep.' I won't speak too soon because I'll ruin it. It's almost like a jinx with kids. When you tell someone they slept through the night, they'll surely not sleep through the night moving forward just to prove you wrong. *Sorry, Mom. You're wrong.*

Wait a minute. I bolt upright, my eyes finally focusing on what's around me. I'm not in my own bed. Then last night's memories flood me. We'd bathed Olive and put her to sleep in Sebastian's bed with a heap of pillows surrounding her. I felt bad taking over his bed, but thankfully, he didn't mind and offered. I remember sitting with him, curled up and tucked under one of his arms. Did he carry me to bed, and I don't remember?

I am definitely in the cabin's bedroom. It's then I register Olive isn't with me and that her laughs are coming from the other side of the door. I've never had anyone get her up for me. Eli wasn't a hands-on dad, ever. He wouldn't change diapers, bathe her, or give her bottles. Even when I was dead on my feet from exhaustion, he wouldn't do it. But he'd be the fun dad and play with her for a little while here and there. He was a good *fun* dad.

Climbing out of bed, I adjust my clothes and straighten them up. I crack the door open, and the smell of pancakes hits my senses, causing my mouth to water. Then I remember I didn't eat last night. Right now, anything would be great, even burned toast.

"Morning, sleepyhead. We've been having a party out here without you," Sebastian greets with a warm grin on his face. Ruby and Olive are on a mat where they're both clutching toast in their little hands, laughing at each other, and trying to share each other's food.

"Sorry for falling asleep last night. I wasn't planning on staying." I rake my hands through my hair, trying to fix it. "You didn't need to take Olive this morning either, but I do appreciate it."

He leaves the frying pan for a moment and comes to me, heat in his eyes. He wraps one arm around my waist and pulls me against him before placing his mouth over mine for a quick morning greeting. "You deserve a sleep-in as well as the next mother. Moms need breaks too, you know." With another dash of a kiss, he releases me and goes back in time to flip the bubbling pancakes.

"Where's Rylee?" I take in the room and register she's missing from the chaos.

"Oh, she'll sleep for another hour or two. She's a very good sleeper. Must get it from her dad because I love a sleep-in, but Anna-Beth? She was an early riser most of the time."

"I can't thank you enough. For last night… for calming me down and just being there for me. It's usually my friend, Isla, who I turn to, but she's a good few hours away."

His focus is on the frying pan. "Even though I was your second option, I think I'll be your first choice from now on." Lifting his head, he winks. My stomach flips like a pancake.

I laugh at his wit. "Maybe you will be, but remember you won't be here much longer." My words bring a weird silence to the room. It's not bad—just weird. I don't want him to leave. I know he'll have to, though, and I'm not sure when that will be. I'm still not sure if it was his wife who saved my life or someone else. Should I tell him I've been thinking about that?

"I wish I could stay," he says softly, pulling me from my thoughts.

"I wish you could as well."

He gets a glass from the cupboard and then pours me a juice. "What should we do?"

I press the rim of the glass to my mouth and pause briefly before taking a small refreshing sip, then swallow and answer, "I don't know."

It's all so new, and I'm not sure I'm ready for a committed relationship. What if I fall head over heels and then end up flat on my butt again, sitting in the mud like I was before he came along and pulled me out?

He's one in a million, but he also has high needs with his girls and his job. I couldn't handle something like that. What the heck am I thinking? We're nothing. We're not going anywhere. It's as if a light bulb lights up above my head, and a sense of dread pours over me like a cold bucket of water. I'm not sure I can do this with him—play happy families.

I move from the bench silently and collect my phone from the coffee table. It's full of missed calls and text messages. I shove it back into my pocket. "Hey, so I think I better get going. It's going to be a big day for me, and I better let you get back to yours without me hassling you with my daughter and family problems." I clear my throat and keep my voice even as I attempt to be casual.

The moment those words leave my mouth, he puts down the egg flipper and comes to stand in front of me. He smells freshly showered, the scent of body wash hits my nose. "What just happened?"

I shake my head, shrugging. "I'm not sure what you mean. I need to go get ready for my day."

His eyes bore into mine. It's clear my casualness didn't faze him. He can see right through my façade. "Don't push me away, Delilah. Please. I'm happy to give you space, but please don't push me away," he says gently.

"I'm not. I just need to process things." Moving around him, I collect Olive and an extra couple of pancakes. "Plus, I've got to get ready to teach little Rylee today. Thanks for last night. It meant a lot to have someone there for me." I give him a chaste kiss and dash out the door into the early morning sunlight that blinds me momentarily. I shield Olive's eyes as her head slams down on my shoulder, and she hides her face in my neck. "Oh, baby girl, you're okay. Let's go get ready for the day. It's going to be a big one."

I'm dreading the confrontation with my family when I get back up to the house. But it needs to happen. We can't walk on eggshells around each other. Not that any of my family members would—we all like to express how we feel most of the time. I've become more reserved about wearing my emotions on my sleeve since keeping what happened to me a secret.

When I finally arrive at the door, voices filter out from inside. My hands tremble, and my body shakes with anticipation. What are they going to say? Will they be mad? I'm sure Tally will have something to say. She always does.

I open the screen and step inside. The voices stop, chairs scrape on the floor, and then footsteps rush to the hallway. Sybil, Tally, and Mabel stop when they see me.

"There's the party girl. Come to Uncle Harley." Harley comes from the living room to my left, claps his hands, and then opens his arms, waiting for Olive. She claps and leans into him, and I let him take her.

"Here. She can have these pancakes, and her sippy cup is in the kitchen."

Harley meets my eyes and gives me a warm smile. He may be a clown on the outside, but on the inside, he's a big softy and always looks out for his sisters.

"Thanks," I say under my breath.

"They're not mad. They just want to talk. Go be sisters and gossip," he says softly with a wink and disappears outside. "Come on, Olive. I'll take you for your first ride on a quad."

My stomach plummets to my feet as I whirl around. "No, you won't," I call out after him.

"Calm down, sis. I'll take her to the baby animals and chickens." He chuckles and says something else that I miss, but Olive seems to love it as she happily claps and then slaps Harley in the face a few times. I chuckle.

I sigh and turn back to my waiting sisters.

"Come on, Dee. We just want to talk," Mabel says gently. My feet start moving, carrying me into the dining room, where there are plates of goodies and steaming cups of coffee on the table.

"How did you know I was coming?"

"Hudson saw you and texted us, so we pulled out what we had," Tally offers, and before I can even turn to look at her, she throws her arms around me. "I'm so sorry for the way I've been acting. I was jealous of what you had. You got to fall in love and leave. I feel trapped here sometimes with no way out, and I know that's not really true, but I'm very sorry for how I've been acting."

She sobs as we hug. Tears stream down my face, and there goes one of the many weights that have been pulling me down.

"It's okay. Sometimes the grass isn't always greener on the other side, but also, don't be afraid to live your life, Tally. You deserve to be happy as much as the next person."

She releases me. "Thank you."

The scent of freshly baked banana bread makes my mouth water. "The bread smells amazing." I pull out a seat and drop into it. There's a small plate in front of me, along with a black mug with a golden rim. "This all looks wonderful. Thanks, girls." I smile at them as they take their seats—Tally and me on one side, Sybil and Mabel on the other.

"Dig in, girls," Tally announces. Glasses clink as we make our coffees. Moments later, our plates are loaded with sweets and warm drinks steaming in front of us.

I take a bite of the warm banana bread and suppress a groan. "This is amazing," I say with a mouthful of food. We continue to fill our bellies until we're all finally sipping on our coffees.

Mabel clears her throat. "Dee, what happened with you and Eli?" Her question is gentle, but all eyes are on me.

Taking one last sip, I fill them in on events with Eli from the moment I left up until the day I arrived home. I don't skip over anything—even the suicide note. I give them the raw version, and when I finish, horror is mirrored on each of their faces. Sybil's hand covers her mouth, and her eyes are wide. Tally's the opposite and appears as though she needs to go a round with a boxing bag to release the tension visible in her shoulders, and she's sitting bolt upright. Mabel hangs her head, and I swear I hear her sob, though she quickly seems to swallow it.

"You don't need to feel sorry for me, girl. It's my own fault," I say.

Tally leaps out of her chair so fast that it tips backward, falling to the floor with a thud. "It is *not* your fault. No one should treat a woman like that. I'm sorry, but I'm glad he's gone, and you're home again."

"Tally," Sybil growls at her. Tally composes herself and removes some of the empty plates from the table, but I still have food on mine which I nibble on.

"Sorry, Dee," Tally says and walks over to the sink.

"What I don't understand is why you never reached out to us. Why didn't you visit or trust us to help you?" Sybil asks with tears in her eyes.

"Because it's a pride thing. I felt ashamed of how my life had turned out. I still do, but I needed to come home. I have been in a bad way since I lost Eli. Isla knew this, and she lied to me to get me to come home. She told me Dad was unwell. So I came home."

Tally rights her chair and takes her seat again, slightly red-faced and not because of embarrassment. Her body is tense, and her eyes are cold. She's always had a temper and becomes super passionate about certain things. Abuse is one of them. "Would you have come home had she not lied to you?"

"Honestly, I'm not sure. I probably would have, but it would've taken me longer to swallow my pride. She knew that. I'm not mad that she lied to me, I'm grateful she did. Being home has helped me."

Sybil takes a sip of her coffee, then says, "I'm glad she lied to you. I can't believe you went through that on your own and didn't tell me, even though you kept in contact. I never once thought you were in trouble. Things sounded wonderful." She stares down into her mug and shakes her head. "I just can't believe it. I wish you'd told us. We're your family."

"I know, and I'm sorry I didn't, but my head wasn't right. Still isn't great but being home and working with horses again is really therapeutic."

"And your health... is it good now?" Mabel asks and points to my chest.

My hand falls where my scar runs. "I'm good. No problems or complications."

Should I tell them about the possibility that it's Sebastian's wife's heart?

"That's good to hear. Well, you're home now. You have to let us h-help you." Mabel's voice catches.

"You all already have by helping me with Olive. Sometimes she's a handful, so having help will take a big weight off my shoulders." I pause then say, "There's something else I need to tell you girls, and I'm not sure if I'm right or not, but since we're being open and honest right now, I have to tell you."

"What's wrong?" Tally asks, her hand reaching to rest on my arm.

I give her a warm smile. "Nothing's wrong, but in the time I've been spending with Sebastian, I've put a few things together." I tell them about Anna-Beth's accident, how Sebastian and I had met in the hospital, and the possibility of having Anna-Beth's heart.

Mabel's eyes go wide, her hand flying to her open mouth, covering it. Sybil doesn't move — just stares at me. Tally's the one who speaks. "Wow, that's crazy if it's true. It's almost like you were meant to come home, and he was meant to be here. That's just… wow. I have no other words for it," she says breathlessly and rubs a hand over her face.

"Yeah, it's a lot, and I've not voiced my thoughts to him obviously because I don't want to upset him or have him hate me."

"That's understandable. So, what are you going to do?"

"Nothing. He has to be the one to want to find out, and then it's all up to him. On the ride we took yesterday, I asked him if he wanted to know, and he didn't seem too concerned." I lift another piece of banana bread to my mouth and take a bite.

"Talk about the story of a lifetime… 'Man falls in love with the woman who has his deceased wife's heart.'" Tally runs her hand in the air and moves it along as though she's reading it off a billboard or something.

"That's nuts," Sybil says. "Don't you think you should at least say something, tell him your suspicions? How do you think he'll react when he finds out that you knew or had some idea about it?"

I shake my head. "No, I don't want to say something it turns out I'm wrong. That would hurt more and I'd have ruined the good friendship we've established."

"An intimate relationship?" Mabel asks with a cheeky grin plastered on her face.

"I'm not sure. Feelings are there, and we've kissed, but nothing more has happened with him, and it may not progress. He's only here for a short while, remember? He could leave any day, and that would be it."

Sybil scrunches up her face. "No way. I'm sure if you both wanted something more, then it could happen."

"That's the thing... I'm not sure I'm there yet. He understands, though, so whatever will be, will be." Even though I'll hate it when he does leave.

My feelings for him are growing. It's exciting and new, but I don't think I can handle a full-on relationship right now. I need a little longer to adjust and actually let go of Eli.

I still have his sealed letter I've never read.

Perhaps it's time to read it and let go.

Chapter 29

Sebastian

STARING DOWN AT MY LAPTOP screen, I see the browser's open to the organ donor recipient information page. There's only one organ I want to know about. I don't need or want to know any others.

My conversation with Mom has been playing on an endless loop in my mind since I woke this morning, and the girls are playing happily for the moment. After Delilah raced out of here today, it crushed me. I felt somewhat whole again having her in here with the girls and me last night. We weren't in the same bed or anything, but having her here, under the same roof, felt really nice.

"Daddy, when are we going horseback

riding?" Rylee asks for what feels like the hundredth time since she woke up.

"I'm waiting to hear from Dee. She'll let me know. Is that okay?"

"Okay, Daddy." She goes back to playing with her dolls, and Ruby watches something on television that has caught her attention.

My phone pings, alerting me to a message. I hit send on the web form before I pick it up to read it. My heart races at the thought of finding out this bit of information. What if it's Delilah who received it? How would that affect us?

She's beautiful, sexy, and smart. I want to know her more and more with each moment I spend with her. I also know that my racing career is a priority, and I'm not sure how the whole thing would work for us if we decided to make a go of something in the future. It's clear she's not ready for a relationship right now. She's still so fragile, and I'd hate to shatter her. Time—that's what she needs.

I pick up my phone. A message lights up my screen, my stomach churns, and an exciting thrill runs through me. It's what I've been waiting for, but why does it give me a feeling of dread?

> **Luke:** Time to pack up your saddle and come home. One of the racers for Haze has gotten himself into some unwanted press, and they're replacing him with you to finish out the season for them.

I hit the call button.

Luke answers immediately. "I hope you're already packing. I worked hard to get them to consider you. Get back here as soon as possible. You better have kept up your training."

"You know me. I'm always in shape and training. I may have slacked off while on holiday, but that's nothing I can't change. What happened to the driver?"

"That's not your concern. Your concern is coming home."

The thought of being back in the car thrills me but saying goodbye to Rose Ridge Ranch and Delilah will be hard. I never planned to find someone like her out here—someone who understands my hurt and my loss. I wish I'd found her long ago or even taken the time to help her more when I saw how distressed she was at the hospital. But I had my own personal things to deal with back then.

It breaks my heart that Ruby will miss the party Mabel has been planning for her and Olive since they're only born a couple of days apart, which is just crazy. The way the world works is mysterious.

"Are you there, Seb?" Luke pulls me back to our conversation. "They've spoken with the FIA, and they're willing to let you race for him and keep his points just to finish out the season. He's not up there in terms of ranking, but it's a chance to show Haze what they've been missing with you not in that seat."

What he's saying makes sense, but now it's all so real. The girls. Delilah. What do I do? I've been waiting for this moment. Mom will be glad to help—she'll happily take care of the girls. Where does that leave Delilah and me? We were getting close, and I don't want to lose that connection.

"Okay, just give me today, and I'll be back tomorrow," I say.

"I'll let them know. See you," Luke says excitedly.

I say goodbye and hang up, staring at the girls who are happily playing. How do I go for my dreams while being a single father with the fear of leaving them left with no one?

"Who was that, Daddy?" Rylee comes to me with a Barbie in one hand and a little brush in the other. Her focus is on getting a knot out of the doll's hair.

"That was Luke."

Her head springs up. "Are you driving again?"

"He asked if I could, yes. Do you think we should do it?"

She frowns. "Does that mean we have to leave?"

"Yes, baby girl, it does. We'd have to leave later today."

With tears in her eyes, she nods. "Okay, Daddy, we can go. Mommy always said you loved racing more than her. She laughed about it."

I pull Rylee into my arms and squeeze her. "I love you and your mother more. You girls are everything to me. Would you like to come with me or stay with Nana? The choice is yours."

"Can we come with you?"

"Of course, you can. I want you girls with me always." I kiss her forehead, and she pulls out of my arms and goes back to her dolls.

I need to talk to Delilah. "Ry, do you want to go up to Mabel at the vacation care for a little while, while I get a few things ready?"

She jumps up and down in one spot. "Yes, yes, yes, please. Maby is fun."

I chuckle and get up. "Okay, let's get you and Ruby ready, and we'll go up there."

"Oh, Daddy, does that mean I don't get to ride the horse?"

My heart drops. "I'll talk to Dee, and maybe she can take you for a quick ride with her. You'll sit on the horse with her. How does that sound?"

Another round of squealed yeses erupts in the tiny cabin.

How is all this going to work? I send off a quick message to Delilah.

> **Sebastian:** *I hope things are okay with you and your family. I'm here if you need me. If possible, can I catch up with you? I need to talk to you about something.*
>
> **Delilah:** *Sure. Everything okay?*

Sebastian: *Yeah.*

Delilah: *Come to the house when you're ready. I'm just doing a job here, and then I plan to take Rylee for her riding lesson.*

Sebastian: *Sounds good to me. See you soon.*

It's not like I can ask her to wait for me or even come with me. She's only just beginning to repair herself and her relationship with her family. Delilah isn't what I expected when I came here.

Chapter 30

Delilah

STANDING OUTSIDE THE LIBRARY, I stare at the worn white door. Many times, I've sat in there with Mom, cried with her, held her hand, and had her comfort me. I can't leave this door shut. It has to be open—not just for me but the family. It needs to become a space of love once again. Mom's library—Mom's space—has been closed off for far too long.

After talking with my sisters this morning, I know this is something that needs to happen. Olive needs this room as much as I did as a kid. If I were in trouble, this is where they'd find me curled up in a corner, either crying or reading one of the many books. Mom made sure there were shelves of books for all our different ages and interests. She was always so thoughtful.

Mabel has taken Olive, which gives me some time. I twist the knob and push the door open. The creak is exactly how I remember it—that sound would let me know Mom was coming into the room. The space is dark, and the curtains are drawn. The dusty scent hits my nose, and a sneeze assaults me.

I walk across the room to the curtains and pull them open one at a time. The sun lights up the room, and memories flood me. Dust is agitated in the air, so I swipe it away. Wow, this room is worse than I thought.

I go to the bookshelves lining the room's walls and pull down the sheets covering them. Old photographs sit in frames on different shelves, but there's no dust. They appear clean. I continue to work my way around and uncover the desk and furniture.

It almost feels back to normal. This room shouldn't be shut off. The memory of Mom fills these walls. I take in the pictures—some are of Mom and Dad, some are the kids, and some are family ones. We had a great childhood, and I wish Mom was here when I was going through the stuff with Dad and Eli, things might have been different. She'd have been more level-headed. She was always better with feelings. Dad wasn't great. He still isn't.

I drop into the couch and take in the room. It's bright and alive again, never to be closed off. I'll have to wipe some of the surfaces down, but it all looks how it should. I remember spending time in here with Eli. We'd talk about our future together and what we both wanted to happen. Our life together didn't resemble those dreams. He was a liar, and I need to work on letting go of those feelings and emotions of hurt he's instilled in me.

I go back to my room and straight to my closet. I pull out a shoebox, go back to the library, and sit in the bay window, taking in the view behind the house. Green stretches across the landscape. There are trees, cattle in the yard, and horses. I can't believe this is my home. An overwhelming feeling of gratitude crashes into me, almost suffocating me. I need to feel these emotions more and not wallow in my past. The past can't hurt me anymore.

I place the box down in front of me on the seat. With trembling hands, I take off the lid to the memories that cause more pain than gratitude. This needs to happen, though. I can't keep holding onto the letter and memories it holds, or it will ruin any chance I have of moving forward with my life.

As I glance inside, the first thing to catch my eye is a photograph of Eli and Olive. This was one of the last pictures I took of the two of them. I can't erase him from her life because he's her dad, and when she gets older, she'll have questions. Most will be hard to answer, but his love for her was different from his love for me. I take the image out and put it aside.

Behind it is a gift—a necklace with the letters D and O on it. I never took it off from the moment he gave it to me. At first, there was just the D charm, and after Olive came along, I went and bought an O—another thing for her. My engagement ring and wedding band are also looped onto the necklace. I'm not even sure why I kept those, but I retained this box for Olive.

I come to the envelope. It's white with off-white corners. My name is penned on it in his neat handwriting. I open it and pull two separate folded pieces of paper out. I release a slow breath. "I can do this."

Slowly, I turn the pages over, and the waterworks start the moment I see my name on one and Olive's on the other. Swiping away the tears, I blink a few times to clear my eyes and set Olive's note aside, then unfold mine.

Dear Delilah,

I don't know where to start. How about an apology? I have never been good at them. I've always been better at blaming and hurting you. For that, I'm sorry. Truly, I am. Sorry for how I treated you. Sorry for abandoning you and Olive. Just sorry.

When you read this, I'll be gone, and you'll be better for it. No more hurt or injury. You and Olive are safe from me now, and I have every hope she'll become the wonderful young woman I know you'll raise her to be.

I'll keep this short.

I'm sorry.
Love,
Eli

A sob tears up my throat. My fist closes and scrunches up the note in my hand. How could he do this? How could he think that his daughter would be better off without him? He may not have been the best husband, but my goodness, I could clearly see his love for her in one single look when he actually took the time with her. I drop the letter to the floor and lean forward, putting my face in my hands.

A light knock at the door startles me. My head shoots up. Sybil stands there with Sebastian behind her, concern etched in the worry lines of his forehead. He rushes past Sybil, whose eyes are transfixed on me as though she can't decide what to do. He pushes the box and contents aside and sits in front of me, his hands taking my face. He studies me a moment before saying, "What's wrong?"

I can't speak. All I can do is point to the floor where the scrunched-up letter now sits.

"Do you need anything, Dee?" Sybil stands beside me, her hand on my back. I'd told them about the letter this morning, and they'd all encouraged me to read it and then get rid of it.

It's not something you need to cling to, they said.

They're right.

Every word I read feels like a lie.

I want to be mad at him for what he's done in abandoning his daughter. I hate him for it. My love for him is still there, but it's not how it was in the beginning—it's about the size of a grain of sand. I'll get through this, and I will raise our daughter to be and do the best she can.

"No, thank you. I'm okay," I whisper.

"I'll be downstairs if you need me."

"Thanks, Sybil."

She leaves and closes the door as she goes. Shutting that would've been smart, then Sebastian wouldn't have witnessed another breakdown of mine.

He removes his hands from my face and picks up the letter. "From Eli? His suicide note?"

I nod.

"What do you want to do with it?"

"I want it gone." It's all I can manage to say.

"Do you want me to get rid of it for you, or we can do it together?"

I shake my head. "No, I'll do it. I have to finish

this chapter of my life on my own. They're emotions I have to feel and move past, and I will. He wrote a note for Olive as well. Will you sit with me while I read it? I thought I could do this on my own, but I like that I don't have to."

"I'm here. Anything you need, I'm here. I won't read it."

Taking another shaky breath, I pick up Olive's note and unfold it. Sebastian rests his hand on my thigh, his comforting grip tight.

My dearest little girl,

I'm sorry I couldn't stay. You were a light in my darkness. Always remember Daddy loves you and will be with you always.

You and Mommy take care of each other. Don't be mad at her for anything—it was all my fault.

I'm sorry I won't be there for your first steps, first day of school, sweet sixteenth, prom, and to walk you down the aisle. I know you'll make great choices. You're your mother's daughter—almost a spitting image.

Love you, little one.

Always.
Daddy

I drop the note, covering my face once again. It's so much to deal with in one day. Dealing with

Eli's stuff drains me, and I have nothing left in my tank. The agony of reading all those sweet things makes me feel sick, but one day she'll ask for something like this. She'll be searching for answers herself.

Sebastian hops up and scoops me into his arms. I curl into his neck. He goes and sits on the couch and holds me tightly against his chest while I cry. Tears fall over him as he runs his fingers through my hair, letting me get out the built-up and stored emotions. I'd kept them tucked away for so long, and now I can't control what my body is going through. It's a mix of shock, hurt, and abandonment.

"It's okay. I've got you," Sebastian comforts me.

Slowly, the sobs stop wreaking havoc on my body, and I fall silent, suddenly exhausted. Why are emotions so tiring?

"I hate feeling like this," I grumble against his chest, his scent calming me as I try to breathe to the rhythm of his breaths. *In through the nose and out the mouth.*

"Feeling those emotions helps you. Trust me." He presses a light kiss to my forehead.

Lifting my head, I meet his gaze. He calms me in ways Eli never could. I want Sebastian in my life. "I'm sure I look horrible, and you're probably sick of me crying on you."

His body shakes as he chuckles. "It's okay. I'm

good with things like this. Emotions don't scare me. In fact, right now, you're helping me because I'm raising two daughters who are going to be *full* of emotions in the coming years," he jokes.

I slap him in the chest and smile. "You're a great dad, and your girls are lucky to have you."

He wipes away the dampness on my cheeks and then slides his hand into my hair, sending goosebumps down my entire body and igniting that flame of passion once again. My mouth seeks his out, and I kiss him hungrily. His lips move as though it's the last time he'll do this. He's so tender and meaningful.

When we come up for air, I stare into his brown eyes. There's something there—he seems off in a way. I climb off his lap and go back to the bay window, picking up the notes from Eli. I scrunch mine into a ball—I'll be burning it later. I don't need to keep this as a reminder. I fold Olive's up and put it inside the envelope again and back in the box, followed by the photograph and necklace.

We remain silent. A ripple of peace crashes into me. It's only a little one, but it's a step in the right direction.

"Thanks for letting me cry on your shoulder *again*. It's been an emotional twenty-four hours for me, that's for sure."

"It's okay. How do you feel about it all?" He hasn't moved from the spot on the couch.

"Better, if that's possible. I'm not carrying extra dead weight with me anymore. When Olive's old enough, I'll talk to her about him, but for now, I don't need to stay stuck in his shadow. He chose to do what he did. That's okay, and I forgive him for everything. I have Olive, and she's all that matters to me."

"You're such a brave woman with so much fire in your heart. Perhaps your new heart has been strong enough to help you get through all of the things you've faced since you received it."

I shrug. "Maybe." Gripping the box, I go to one of the bookshelves and reach up and put it up high. Now it'll be out of sight and mind until the day Olive asks about him. I turn and study Sebastian. He fidgets with his fingers in his lap as his eyes dart around the room.

"Something's wrong, and it's not me crying here right now?" I have a feeling what this could be about. He got the call he's been waiting for — it's written all over his face, and the sadness in his eyes slams into me. I knew this would possibly come, now it has, and I'm not sure how to feel.

Chapter 31

Sebastian

"YOU'RE RIGHT. SOMETHING IS UP," I say and stand from my spot on the couch. I'd much rather sit there all day with her, comforting, cuddling, and kissing her. Being so close to her is soothing and settling. Thoughts of her consume me.

She takes a seat at the window again, clearly a favorite spot of hers. "You're leaving. You got the call you've been waiting for," she states with a small smile.

"How?" I ask. She's caught me off-guard.

"I'm taking a guess here. Am I right?"

I move to sit beside her and take her hand in both of mine. "I don't want to leave. I wanted to spend more time with you. I wanted Rylee to have some lessons. Even though this is what I've been waiting for, it's come at a time when I'm struggling to want to go. Something is holding me here, and that's you." I never thought I'd say that sentence, but Delilah has taken hold of my heart, and I don't want her to let go.

She places her hand on top of mine, holding hers. "This is who you are. You need to go and win those races. I'm sure it's what Anna-Beth would want you to do."

"What about you?" I ask.

She smiles, and her eyes light up shimmery blue because of her freshly fallen tears. "I'll be okay. This isn't about me. It's all about you and the girls."

"You're right, but I can't help wanting to stay with you. You've had this hold over me from the moment we met in front of the barn. Everything about you captivates me. You're amazing, and I don't want to be away from you. Would you consider coming with me?"

Her eyes widen, and she leans back a little but doesn't pull away. "I'd love to, but I can't. I need to be here with Olive for a little while. I need to recharge my batteries and fix a relationship with my father that's been broken for the last three years." She pauses a moment. "You go do you, and I'll be here when and if you still want. Either way, I'll be okay."

Delilah's words seep into my bones. It's not the answer I want, but it's the right one. I know it, and obviously, she does as well. I don't want to accept it, though. I wish she had said yes and was coming with me.

"I don't want to leave you," I say softly as I press my forehead to hers.

"It gives me a chance to grow and learn to be on my own. We can always call and message when you're free, and maybe this could be a test."

"A test?" I echo.

"Yeah. If these feelings are still there after some time apart, we can try to make something of them, but I think, for now, this might be for the best." Her eyes shimmer with more tears, and a weak smile spreads across her face.

"If that's what you'd like, I'm happy to give it a go."

"Whatever happens, happens for a reason. You go win these races and prove to all of them that you've still got it. This is who you are. Don't change that for anyone, except maybe your girls. They're the only ones who get a choice." She squeezes my hands. It's comforting.

"You're right. Can you do me one favor, though?"

"Sure. What's that?"

"Can you take Rylee for a ride with you on the horse, please? She's been begging me about riding lessons, and maybe hopping on with you will be good enough until we get back here in the future."

I don't plan to stay away.

Delilah is here, and this is where I'll return to.

I'll come back for her.

She laughs, and it's music to my ears. "I'd be happy to take her. I'll let her ride on her own as well, but I'll hold the reins. That should tide her over until she comes back."

"She'd love that." I give Delilah one last chaste kiss. "Do you want some help in here for a bit? Rylee wanted to see Mabel, so the girls are down there with her. I saw Olive there as well. She's fitting in perfectly."

"She's going to be very bored when your girls leave. There are other kids around but none her age. I'm sad Ruby will miss her birthday party the girls have been planning."

"Yeah, me too."

She pops up out of her seat. "I've got an idea. Come on. I can finish this later. It's not going anywhere, but you are. Come on. I need to talk to Mabel."

Chapter 32

Delilah

AN HOUR AFTER TALKING WITH Mabel, Mabel's taken it upon herself to bring the party forward to today. In just a few hours. She's got Tally on food duty, and thankfully, she has pre-baked a lot of things. There's plenty of candy and chocolate in the cupboard since we're a houseful of girls, and the candy and chocolates are needed. Mabel has sent Hudson and Harley to do the rounds and get the family together, along with any other families who want to participate.

"Don't worry. Things are going to be great. You two go play with the horses. I'll get all this ready for your return," Mabel assures Sebastian and me.

We collect Rylee from vacation care and take

her to Butter's pen. Butter was saddled up and ready to go.

"Oh, so pretty. I'm so excited," Rylee squeals with a little jump and stomp of her feet. The dust stirs beneath her.

I drop down to Rylee's level, take the helmet I have tucked under my arm, pop it onto her head, and tighten it. "Now you have a choice. You can ride Butter with me, and we can go a little bit faster, or we can walk Butter around on the lead with you on your own in the saddle. What do you want to do?"

She hasn't been able to wipe the smile off her face. She glances up at her dad.

He says, "This is your choice, Ry."

Rylee shrugs her shoulders high and keeps them there while she bows her head. "I'd like to do both, please."

"You know what, Rylee? I think we can," I say. Her shoulders relax right away. "Which one do you want to do first?"

"Can I go with you first?"

"Of course, you can." I hold my hand out to her, and she takes it willingly. We open the gate to Butter's pen, and he neighs a greeting. Rylee giggles.

"He's saying hello. That's why we named him Butter. He melts everyone as easily as butter. Plus, he loves little kids," I say.

"How come you don't wear a helmet?" she asks.

"Well, I'm a little older, and I've been riding since I was your age. My mom and dad taught me all I know about horses, and I'll teach you what they taught me and all that I've learned myself. How does that sound?"

"Great."

We stop at Butter and scratch him on the nose and neck. Sebastian has been following closely behind us but keeping quiet.

"All right, I need you to hold Dad's hand while I climb on, and then he'll pass you up to me," I say, and she nods. With one swift move, I hook my foot into the stirrup and then hoist myself up easily. Butter doesn't move as I adjust myself. He's so well trained.

"Wow." Rylee beams.

"Now it's your turn," Sebastian says as he lifts her to me. I take her leg and guide it over the saddle so she's got one leg on either side. We adjust ourselves until we're comfortable.

"I'm up really high," she gushes.

"Yes, you are, baby girl," Sebastian says with a tear in his eye.

"Hold on here." I place her hands on the horn, keeping her tucked tightly between my arms as I hold the reins.

"Look this way. Let me get a photo," Sebastian

says. Rylee and I turn to him and give him our best grins. Holding up his phone, he then says, "Perfect."

"Ready?" I ask Rylee.

"Yes," she responds eagerly. I click my tongue. Butter starts forward, and with a little push from my legs, he speeds up—only a little, though. I'm not going to let loose with Sebastian's daughter on here with me.

We spend the next hour out here. We do a little bit of riding with me, and then Rylee rides on her own. Sebastian watches close by and snaps lots of photographs. His smile hasn't left his face, and neither has Rylee's. I'm glad I can do this for her and give her good memories to keep forever.

When we're finished, I lead Butter back to his stall, and Rylee helps me take his saddle off, freshen up his water, and top off his food. "You're such a good helper, Rylee," I say as I brush down Butter. It's always important to teach kids how to care for the horse—not just ride it.

I glance over my shoulder to Sebastian, whose eyes bore into mine. Something silent passes between us, and I hate that I feel as though each hour that passes by is going to be our last. The moment he leaves, I may be erased from his thoughts. What he says and what he actually does may be two different things, and only time will tell how things will play out between us. I do need to find myself and rediscover who I am. I spent so long in Eli's shadow—now it's time for me to rise from the dark pit of despair and live and find love again. If that's with Sebastian, then things will work out. If they don't, then that's okay too.

We arrive at Mabel's vacation care room which is now transformed into a party zone. Balloons are scattered over the floor and stuck to the walls and corners of the room. Colored streamers go from one side of the room to the other.

"Wow," Rylee whispers and runs off through the room of balloons and right to Ruby, sitting in a highchair that has streamers dangling from the ends of the tray. Olive sits in one right beside her.

"Don't they look adorable?" I gush at the girls. Both squeal with delight as Rylee dances in front of them and throws balloons in the air around them.

"They are," Sebastian says, almost in a whisper.

To the left of the room, there's a table full of food. Tally has been busy. "Come get some of these cookies I just spotted. They're delicious... Tally makes them." I hook my arm in his and pull him to the table of goodies.

We load up some little pink party plates, head to our girls, and stand beside them, feeding our faces. "Gee, my sisters know how to throw a party," I say.

He nods, taking a bite of a cookie. "They really do."

"Smile," Sybil says as she stands in front of us with a camera. "Get closer and smile." We shuffle closer, our arms touching. Sybil holds the camera up and snaps a few pictures. "Now, go stand with the girls so we can get Sebastian, Ruby, and Rylee, and then you can get a photo with Olive if that's okay?" We both nod and set about getting the images she wants.

When she walks away, Sebastian has become noticeably quiet. After we put the girls on the floor to crawl around and play, I face him. "Are you okay?"

Clearing his throat, he says, "I just need a minute." And then he walks out of the building. I stare after him.

Mabel comes up beside me. "Is he all right?"

I shrug. "I'm not sure. Things were fine, and then just now, he's changed. Perhaps it has something to do with his wife… that's all I can put it down to. I'll go talk to him, and then we can get ready to do the cake if that's okay. He's got to get back to town to sort out his racing."

"Yeah, not a problem. I get it. I'll get things sorted in here. You go to him." Mabel walks toward the table, and I head in Sebastian's direction.

Outside, I find him sitting on the bottom step of the building. I make my way to him and drop down beside him. "Want to talk about it?"

He's silent for a beat, and when I chance a glance at him, tears glitter in his eyes that he quickly wipes away. "Sorry," he mutters and keeps wiping the moisture away.

I wrap my arm around his shoulders and pull him against me. "It's okay." I comfort him. We remain like this for a couple of minutes while I wait for him to speak.

"Anna-Beth should've been here for this. She's been gone a year, and as much as I don't want Ruby's birthday to be a constant reminder of our loss, I'm worried I'll be horrible at making Ruby's day special because of my own feelings." He pauses, clearing his throat. "I know it's not Ruby's birthday today, but when it comes, I'm not sure what to do about my feelings of loss while trying to enjoy Ruby's happy moment." His eyes meet mine, and tears pool in mine.

I do the one thing I can think of at this moment—I pull him into a hug. As we hold each other, I say, "It's okay to have those feeling and to miss Anna-Beth. You should celebrate Ruby and mourn Anna-Beth, though I know both of those are complete opposites. But it's also good for the girls to remember their mom. Not that I ever think you'll *not* talk about Anna-Beth. Oh, I'm messing this up."

We release our hug, but he keeps a hold of my hand. "No, you're not. I get what you're saying."

"You could celebrate Ruby's birthdays along

with Anna-Beth's life, not her loss," I say when I finally get my words to work better.

Lifting my hand, he presses a kiss on the back of it. "Thank you. I know this may not be a comfortable conversation for you to have with me, but I appreciate it."

"Hold on. Did you happen to miss my suitcases of baggage coming in hot behind me?" I joke, and he laughs, squeezing my hand. "I'm the queen of not unpacking baggage."

"Perhaps I was brought here for a reason, and meeting you was that reason."

I grin, unable to settle the swirling of happiness in my stomach. "Maybe we're here to help each other."

"I think there's more to this than just being there for each other." He gestures between us.

"I have to agree with you. Things happen for a reason, and I'm glad you came because you've helped me, even though you may not realize it." Leaning over, I press a kiss to his cheek, and we sit there a moment.

Finally, he says, "Should we go back in before they send a search party?"

"Probably. Knowing Mabel, she'll have one of the girls looking for us shortly."

We get up from the step, and I start to head inside when he takes my arm, pulling me against his chest. I wrap my arms around him and listen to the sounds of the birds and horses in the nearby stalls.

"Thank you for everything. You have no idea how much just being near you has helped me, and I want to stay, but I know I need to do this for me," he says into my hair, his breath tickling my neck.

"You've helped me as well. I can't thank you enough for being there when I needed someone."

"Look at us… two broken souls mending each other in different ways," he says and releases me but takes my hand, leading me back inside.

The afternoon goes so fast, and before long, I stand at the driver's side door of Sebastian's car with Olive on my hip. Sebastian buckles the girls in, and I'm holding back tears. I don't want him or the girls to go. Connecting with him has been a highlight of my return home, apart from catching up with family. Dad still hasn't spoken to me since I got mad at him. Now that I think about it, I've not seen him at all except for when he showed up in the back of the room today as we sang "Happy Birthday" to Olive and Ruby. He left as quickly as he came in.

We need to talk, but he has to come to me. I can try with him, but as Mom would say, he's stubborn and pigheaded sometimes. He'll figure it out, though, and when he does, I'll be here, ready and waiting to talk to him.

Sebastian shuts the door and turns to face me.

He rubs his hand on his pants and moves closer to Olive and me. "I really don't want to leave."

I take a step toward him, our bodies now inches apart. His arm wraps around my waist and pulls me against him. "I know you don't, and I don't want you to go. You have to do this, though. I'll be watching and cheering you on. But don't do anything stupid. You hear me?" I poke him in the chest with my finger.

His grip tightens on Olive and me. "I'll do what I need to."

"And that's what frightens me because I know the kind of driver you are. I was watching you before you stopped. You were one of my favorites."

Sebastian's eyebrow cocks up. "Really?" he teases.

"Yes, really. Don't get too excited. Promise me something?"

"What's that?"

I move my face close to his, my lips hovering over his mouth. "That you'll try to come back to me. I know I said earlier, whatever happens will happen, but I'd like you to try to keep that promise."

He closes the gap, his warm lips tasting mine.

The heat.

The passion.

The promise in one kiss.

We pull away, breathing heavily.

Olive smacks my face. It's not really romantic. "I guess she's not ready to share," I say, giving her a cheeky smile which she returns.

"She'll have to get used to it," Sebastian says. After one last kiss, he places a small peck on Olive's head, climbs into his car, and drives off down the road, taking some of my heart with him.

Chapter 33

Delilah

"YOU READY TO GET YOUR butt beat?" Harley attempts to goad me as we saddle up the horses for our ride. I think he's really trying to help take my mind off Sebastian leaving about an hour ago.

"You realize who you're up against, don't you?" I mock while tightening the saddle's strap.

"Ha, you're out of practice. I've got this in the bag."

This is something we always used to do. There's a track we would use and race around the paddock on the horses, going as fast as we could, trying to beat each other. We were so competitive with each other.

I test the straps and then hastily get up on Holly while Harley does the same with his horse,

Buster, who's an ex-racehorse. He still has so much talent—he used to have the wrong owner until I found him, trained him, and gave him the love he deserved.

"Let's go," I say. With a click of my tongue, Holly leaps forward, and I guide her out of the barn and down the same road Sebastian and I went down yesterday. I only walked with Sebastian to the start of our track as he isn't as experienced as Harley and me.

Once we hit the dirt track out in the paddock, Harley and I both give a nudge with our feet into the horses' bellies, and they take off. Their hooves clap along, and it's music to my ears. The adrenaline pumping through me brings the biggest smile to my face. I've missed this. Trees and fences blur past us. When we get to the creek, we wade across it and surge forward to the open field where cattle are grazing with some other horses. Our property boundary is in the distance, and it's a race to see who gets there first.

Harley comes up beside me, but little does he know, Holly isn't at her hardest clap yet. I know how to manage her pacing and make it appear as if she's going all out, but in fact, she's not. As he pushes past us and the fence line comes into view, I mutter, "Let's go, girl."

I give her a fast push, and we power past the stunned Harley, his eyes wide as he shakes his head and laughs loudly.

I arrive at the fence before Harley, and Holly huffs out a breath. "Good job, girl." I climb off and lead her to the water trough. When Harley arrives, he does the same.

"I kicked your butt," I say.

"It's like you hit the fast button, and she shot off."

"Yeah, it's our secret weapon." I run my hand down Holly's neck, then turn to stare back from where we came. The homestead is a little dot in the distance. There's so much room and space here. To the left out farther, there's a rundown house from the first family who lived there. It's a small piece of history for us that we can't seem to tear down.

A spine-chilling scream rips through the silence. My stomach drops. It's like something you'd hear in a thriller movie. Harley and I spin in the direction the cry came from on the opposite side of the fence.

"What was that?" he asks as we both scan the area.

A blur in the distance captures my attention. Pointing, I say, "Look! Over there."

Before I can gather my reins, Harley is on his horse and taking off for the gate leading to the neighbor's paddock. Finally, when I manage to get myself organized, I'm on the back of Holly, following him. Harley leans over, unhooks the gate, and takes off. I close it when I pass through and gallop after him. I see the blur in the distance still. Harley must as well because that's where he's heading.

When I get close, I notice a tall, dark-haired girl on the back of a black-as-night mustang. What the hell is she doing on the back of one of those? Dotty, the neighbor, is known to have wild ones on her property to be trained.

Harley manages to get alongside the horse, grab its reins, and pull it to a stop. The minute he gets the horse to halt, the girl is off its back and collapsing on the ground. I leap off Holly and race to her, knowing Holly won't go anywhere.

"Are you okay?" I drop down beside her. When her head comes up and her eyes meet mine, fear stares back at me. It sends a chill down my spine. What would've happened had Harley and I not been here?

I reach for her. She screams. "Get away from me! Don't touch me." She goes to get up and move away, but she stumbles back right into Harley's arms while he still grips the mustang's reins. The horse startles, then she does as well.

"It's okay. We're not here to hurt you," he says gently and helps her to her feet. He follows her moves and glances up and down at her, possibly checking to see if she's hurt.

The woman breathes heavily. "I don't want your help."

"This horse isn't good to be ridden, it's clearly

not trained. Any person out here knows that. You must be new around these parts," Harley says, but he isn't being nasty. He genuinely wants to make sure she's okay. She looks at me, then Harley, like a frightened animal.

I hold my hands out in front of me. "Let us help you get back home. Do you live in the house on this property?"

Her eyes dart between Harley and me, then she stops on me. "Y-Yes. I'm visiting." Her words are breathless and shaky.

"Can we help you get home?"

She shakes her head. "No. I can get there on my own."

"What are you doing on this horse? It's nowhere near trained. They're usually wild horses around here," Harley says and admires the black horse in front of him, gripping its lead. "If you want, we could work with him for a bit and then bring him back when he's in a better place to be ridden on."

"I don't want the horse," she snaps and wobbles off in the direction of the house on the property, wearing a tight blue shirt and short jeans. Clearly, not a girl from around here.

Harley and I glance between each other, then say, "City girl."

It's clear she's not familiar with horses. Any person who lives in these parts would easily have seen how unsteady this animal is. It's a beauty, though, and I see through its skittish exterior. It has a lot of potential in its eyes.

"Let's take the horse home," I say and climb back on Holly who's grazing.

Harley throws a thumb over his shoulder. "What about her? We can't just leave her out here."

"Harley, she doesn't want our help. What more can we do?"

"I'm going to take the horse back to the neighbor, and I'll try to get her to talk to me."

"Good luck with that. She's clearly frightened of something. I say leave her to settle down. I'll give Dotty a call when I get home to find out if everything is okay. She always seems to take in the strays around here."

"Okay, I'll make sure she gets home, and you do that."

"See you at home." He leads both his horse and the mustang in the direction the girl is going. It's clear something is bothering her. She didn't want to be touched or assisted in any way. The fear she had in those dark eyes is something I felt when I was with Eli. What's her story?

Chapter 34

Delilah

Two weeks later

"COME ON, HARLEY. YOU'RE GOING to miss it," I call to him in the kitchen as I sit in the living room with the television on the racing.

It's been hard not talking to Sebastian much these last two weeks, but when I do hear from him, it sets butterflies off in my stomach. He's made sure to reach out if he hasn't heard from me in a while.

"Yeah, yeah. I'm coming." Harley comes into the room with his arms full of packets of sweets and a big bowl of popcorn. Olive is asleep in my bedroom.

"Has it started yet?" Mabel and Sybil come in and take a seat beside me.

"Not yet. I'm so nervous for him. I can't even imagine how he's feeling." I pull out my phone and send him a quick text, knowing he probably won't get it until after the race.

> **Delilah:** *Good Luck. I'm so happy for you to be doing what you love again. You've got this. Thinking of you xx*

"Do you mind if I join?"

All heads turn toward Dad standing in the doorway at the hallway entrance. He still hasn't spoken to me about Eli or my health since that night, but we have been nicer to each other.

"Hey, girls, can you help me get some more snacks? I don't think I've gotten enough," Harley not so subtly suggests, glaring at my sisters. All of them have been doing this lately, somewhat forcing Dad and me to talk. They all scurry off as Dad comes and sits in his usual worn brown recliner.

"How much longer do you think they're going to do this?" he mutters as he settles back into his seat.

"Until it stops feeling as though they're walking on eggshells when we're in the same room." I pause and stare at him, take a break, and continue, "I'm still not sure where I stand with you. I forgive you for how you spoke to me that night. I just wish you had come to me instead of blurting it out in front of the whole family."

"Well, I guess now is the time for that talk. I was hoping it would be forgotten."

"You can't be serious, Dad. You were pretty nasty toward me."

He hangs his head, and my stomach knots. I hate making my dad feel bad, but he needs to know how he made me feel. "I know, and for that, I'm very sorry. I've never been good with feelings and emotions. Your mother was the one who I always relied on for advice."

"I know that. Dad, why didn't you just pick up the phone after I left? We could've spoken about everything then. You hurt me so much, and I want to forgive you for all of it, but how can I when we don't talk?" I grip my hands in my lap and turn to face him.

He stares ahead. "I didn't want to lose you. I'd already felt so alone since your mother died, and the thought of losing one of my children? The fear took over, and I didn't handle it very well. And Eli..." he sighs, rubbing his eyes, ". . . I knew he wasn't right, but I couldn't stop him or you. Once you made your mind up on something, that was it. You're every bit like your mother in that way."

"Do you think we can move forward from all of this stuff?" I ask. "No more snaps. No more judging and no more trying to run things in my life. If I make mistakes, I make them. It's nothing on you."

"Delilah, I know that. I think I can manage all of that. Your mistakes are your own. No more judgment."

I get up from my spot on the three-seater couch and go to him. Leaning over, I hug him, a lump forming in my throat. "I love you, Dad. Even if you're a stubborn man."

"I love you too, Delilah. I care for you, which is why I sometimes do stupid things. Thank you for forgiving me, and I'm glad you came home. I love having everyone here, but I know the time will come when everyone goes their own way. I guess as a father, the thought of not having anyone scares me."

My heart skips a beat at Dad's admission. "It's okay, Dad. I guess I'll find out myself what that fear is like in the coming years." I release him and go back to my seat.

"The girls told me everything. I'm sure you would've told me yourself when we had this talk, but they didn't want you rehashing it again. I'm sorry I wasn't there for you to turn to. I'm glad Isla told a white lie to get you home. I'll have to send her flowers."

We laugh. "I'm sure she'd love that. Thanks, Dad. Things can only improve now, can't they?"

"That's right. Now we just have to get through Sebastian's race, and I'm nervous." He runs his hand through his hair and releases a breath.

"You and me both. He's a good guy, Dad."

"I know he is. I can see how he is with his girls and even the way he treated you and looked after you when you were upset. He cares for you, as do we all."

"Thanks, Dad."

"Is it safe to come out now?" Harley calls from the kitchen. "We don't want to miss the race."

"Yes," Dad and I both say in unison.

"Hey, Harley, have you heard anything from that girl from next door since we helped her?" I ask.

"No, something's not right there. No matter how much I offered to help, she wasn't very nice. I popped over yesterday, and Dotty told me she didn't want me to come around to see the girl anymore. She was nasty for an elderly lady."

Dad glances in his direction. "Dotty said that to you? She has no right to talk to you like that. You were just being nice and checking on the girl."

We all pass a look at each other before Harley says, "It's okay. I won't bother her anymore. It was clear she was shaken by something but is good at biting heads off when she's angry."

"Maybe Dotty will talk to me," I offer.

"Don't waste your breath on that woman," Dad says like he's suddenly turned into a grumpy old man.

"Why, Dad?" I probe.

"Forget I said anything. Look, the race is almost about to start." He points to the screen.

My attention is drawn back to the television. Sebastian is in pole position. He sits in his car, helmet on, staring ahead—focused and determined. He cleaned up in qualifying even after tapping the wall. He still managed to get a great lap time for his first time back on the track. I may have died a little when he did that. This is so different for me to watch now because I know Sebastian and care for him deeply. I'm more scared of something happening to him. Before, I'd fear for the drivers but in a different, disconnected way.

Mabel, Sybil, Harley, Tally, Hudson, Odette, and Devon settle into their seats. We're all here together and watching what we all enjoy, although the boys think they could race too. They clearly don't understand the training involved, but that's boys for you.

On the screen, the racers do their formation lap, zigzagging over the track to heat up their tires. My hands fidget and then cover my face as they get to the line-up. The lights go out. "I can't watch."

I peek through my fingers at the screen. Sebastian has the fastest take-off and makes the first corner after incredibly close contact with another car, but it's nothing too bad. I hold my breath as I wait to see how things pan out during the first few laps.

An hour or so later, my nerves are shot, and my stomach is a pile of knotted ropes. Sebastian has raced amazingly, even if he came in second.

It's better than last, and he looks thrilled, holding his trophy up high, the crowd cheering for him. We all scream and cheer for him too. Our house sounds like it's the site of a massive party.

"What a race," Mabel says with a sigh as though she's just released her breath. I felt as though I held mine for the entire race.

I love that man.

I don't care what anyone says — *I love him.*

Chapter 35

Sebastian

Two weeks later

THAT'S TWO FOR TWO. NOTHING could wipe this smile off my face. The moment I've done my media duties, I go to get dressed. My girls and mother are waiting for me in the change rooms. Their screams of joy fill me with so much happiness. There's only one—no, two people missing—Delilah and Olive. Phone calls and texts aren't enough.

"We're so proud of you, Seb," Mom gushes and rushes to me, wrapping me in her arms, squeezing tightly.

"Thanks, Mom." She lets go, and I drop to my knees and smother the girls in kisses. Two second places in four weeks. This is more than I could've hoped for on my return to racing. Luke has been talking with other teams seeking me to join them next year, but I haven't made any decisions yet. I have missed this thrill for so long. Now I'm back in the seat behind the wheel, I'm more determined than ever to go for that championship.

"Your phone went off a few times." Mom nods to the table where my stuff sits, and I reach for it, knowing who it will be.

> **Delilah:** Good luck. You got this. Always thinking of you xx

> **Delilah:** You're amazing. I'm so happy for you, but I'll admit that I miss you and the girls. You also aren't gaining points when you send my heart into a tailspin. You'll send me to my grave early.

I chuckle at the last sentence. She exaggerates so much.

"Is that Delilah?" Mom asks.

"Yeah. Grilling me because I'll send her to an early grave."

"I worry about the same thing. I know you love this, but son, my heart can't stand it when I watch sometimes."

I close the message as I'll reply after I get changed and refreshed. I notice a few emails in my inbox that I've neglected lately because I've been trying to get back up to speed. I'm frazzled with so much going on with the girls, meetings, and the media. I forgot how busy things are when I'm on the road.

"All right, girls, let's give Dad a minute. We can go for a little walk and see Uncle Reuben." The girls cheer with delight. Even Ruby who knows exactly who Uncle Reuben is.

"Thanks, Mom. I'll take a shower and come find you."

"Take your time, honey." She takes their little hands in her caring ones and leads them out, and I'm left to have a moment of silence to myself and reflect on what happened today. I placed second again, and I couldn't be happier with my performances over the last two races. There are a few more to go, but thankfully, I have a three-week break between now and the next race.

Perhaps I could go to see Delilah for a week in there. I want nothing more than to hold her in my arms and kiss her nonstop for like twenty-four hours. Give us a hotel to ourselves and a babysitter for the night. I love her, but I'm not saying it over text messages or phone calls. As the saying goes, distance makes the heart grow fonder, and I couldn't be fonder of Delilah. She makes me laugh and fully supports me.

I go to my phone and tap the inbox app. About fifty emails pop up. My mouth drops open, and I start deleting all the usual junk emails. I'm about to delete one I don't recognize when I spot the words *organ donation*.

Holding my breath, I open it.

Hello Mr. King,

We are greatly sorry for your loss and thankful to your wife for her donations, which helped save many lives that day. I know you asked about the recipient of her heart and nothing else. After talking with people higher than myself, we are able to give you that information but ask if you wish to contact the person, you must go through us. The patient's name is:

Delilah Olive Reily

I stop reading.

The rest of the email is pointless to me now.

My entire body feels as though it's shaking. It's her. She has Anna-Beth's heart. Is this the reason I'm drawn to her? That she interests me? That can't be it. My feelings for her are real, and nothing can change them.

But knowing she has a part of Anna-Beth brings tears to my eyes.

The door opens, and I rush to swipe away the tears. I still sit on the floor where the girls left me.

"Sorry, honey. I forgot my purse. The girls wan—" Mom cuts her words off and she's by my side instantly. "What's wrong?"

I can't seem to form the words, so I hold out my phone and show her the email.

Her hand flies to her mouth. "Oh, my."

Swallowing, I say, "What do I do, Mom? I love this girl, but is it only because of the heart?"

Mom takes my hand, tears glittering in her eyes. "Honey, that's not why you love her. You fell in love with her as a person. She was this person before she met you, and her family knew who she was before her transplant. It's all her. Anna-Beth's spirit is gone, but she helped Delilah live so she could find you and make you happy. Make you both happy again after such losses. You need to go to her right away. Don't wait. Tell her you love her and tell her about the transplant."

Chapter 36

Delilah

HE DIDN'T MESSAGE OR CALL me back. It's been almost twenty-four hours. He usually rings me after he gets the girls down on race day. This is weird.

I work with Diamond, who has come a long way over the last couple of weeks. She's letting me on her back now, and she's calm when I pet her. Sudden movements still startle her, so I have to be mindful of those. Gently, I brush her down and talk to her.

"He didn't ring me last night, Diamond. It's weird, and it makes me wonder if I've been forgotten." I love talking to her about Sebastian. She doesn't have an opinion, and I don't have doubtful thoughts put into my head after we speak.

"Do you think the time is up for us now? Perhaps he found some hot girl at the track and now she's more important."

"No one is more important than you, Delilah."

I whirl around to the sound of Sebastian's voice. "What the? Why are you here?"

"I came for you."

I rush out of Diamond's pen, dropping the brush. I leap into Sebastian's arms, my legs wrapping around his waist as I inhale his familiar scent. My body ignites with want, desire, and overwhelming love for this man. His hot breath hits my ear.

"I love you, Delilah. You're everything to me and all I want for the rest of my life." He sets me down, our mouths crash together, and the world fades away. The worry I held within me disappears.

"I love you too," I say between heated kisses.

We become lost in each other, exploring and caressing body parts that haven't been touched in such a long time—my heart, for example. It hasn't been easy, but the future looks bright, and I couldn't be more ecstatic to see what life brings with Sebastian.

He stops the kissing and says, "There's something I need to tell you."

"Okay," I say warily. What could he possibly have to say after I love you? Was he buttering me up for something worse?

"It's about your heart transplant."

"Oh, I think I already know. Not for sure, but I kind of put it together," I jump in and admit.

Sebastian's head rears back, but he doesn't let me go. "You knew and didn't say anything?"

"No, it wasn't my place, and I figured you'd look into it at some stage. I wasn't hiding it from you, I just didn't know for sure. Did you look into it?"

He nods.

"And?"

Tears fill his eyes, and that gives me my answer before he has to say anything. "You have Anna-Beth's heart," he chokes out, and I pull him back into my arms as he sobs on my shoulder.

"It's okay. I've got you." We stand like this for a while as he silently cries. "I love you, Sebastian," I finally say.

Clearing his throat, he says, "I love you too. I'm not upset or anything. I'm grateful for you and for the person you are. You were put in my path, and for that, I'm so happy. I'm thrilled I have you in my life now and in the future.

"I know this isn't conventional and may seem a little crazy, but I know in my heart it's you I want to be with for the rest of my life. I lost one person I cared deeply about, and I found you later down the track. I understand if you say no, but please, really consider it."

What's he going on about? It's all romantic and stuff, but where's he going with this speech?

As if in a Hallmark movie, he digs in his pocket and then drops down on one knee. My mouth drops, and my hands fly to cover it. "What are you doing?" I cry as tears fill my eyes.

"I'm wondering if you'll marry me? It doesn't have to happen anytime soon. But I want you to be mine, and I'll gladly be yours if you'll have me?" His dark eyes hold mine captive.

I start to give him the answer I want to scream and then pause. "It's not because of Anna-Beth's heart that you're doing this, is it?" I ask, and I'm sure I sound stupid, but I need to know.

He frowns. "No. Not a chance. I fell in love with you before I even knew about the heart. I grew to love you as the person you are, not because of anything else. You're my present and future. What do you say?" He stays on one knee.

I nod furiously. "Yes, I will." Tears slide down my cheeks as he places the princess-cut diamond ring on my wedding finger and then scoops me up in his arms, spinning me around.

Claps fill the little barn.

My family stands in the doorway, Dad included. They were in on this, and they're happy for me.

I couldn't be more excited for the future and what it holds for both of us. I love Sebastian with my whole heart.

Epilogue

Harley

"Why are you even bothering with Dotty again?" Delilah asks as she packs hers and Olive's suitcase to go with Sebastian.

"Because I feel I need to. I don't know why, and I can't explain it," I reply.

I never expected Sebastian to propose, but he came here and wanted to talk to all of us—especially Dad. He told us his intentions and the information he'd discovered about his late wife and Delilah. It actually brought a tear to our old man's eyes. Dad couldn't tell him no after that. He told Sebastian to make sure she came home often. Sebastian's response was, "We'll be home when we don't need to be on the track, or whenever Delilah wants to come home, she can. I'm never going to stop her." And that made Dad happy.

"Harley, can you make sure that Dad doesn't close the library up? I don't want to come home and find that door shut again. You hear me?" Her head comes up, and her hard eyes bore into mine.

"Yes, boss. We won't close the doors again. I promise, especially since you'll be coming home," I say, and she goes back to her closet to grab some clothes.

"Yes, I will be." She stops packing and stares at me. "Am I doing the right thing, or am I rushing into this?"

I shrug. "I can't answer that... only you can. And you're not running off and getting married this instant, are you?"

She shakes her head. "You're right. I should just see what happens. I'm happy, and that's what matters."

"That's what matters," I agree.

"Now, about Dotty. Just forget about the girl and what Dotty has said."

"I can't get her out of my head. It's driving me crazy. It's stupid, I know, but I want to know that she's okay and at least get her name." Since I met the mystery neighbor, she's all I can think about. Only a crazy person takes an untamed mustang and attempts to ride it.

"I went and saw Dotty a few weeks back to check on the girl because you wouldn't shut up about her, and she said the girl is only visiting for a little while. You know her, she likes to be up in everybody's business but won't let anyone, especially our family, close to her. I'm surprised she didn't pull a gun on you when you took the girl home. She's been known to do that in the past."

While walking home with the girl, I'd asked questions like her name. She gave me the letter M, and that was it. When we got close to the house, she took off at a run and didn't stop until she was through the back door. Dotty was waiting at the fence line, her brows furrowed and that familiar grouchy look on her face. It's like a permanent expression for her. She doesn't let anyone in or near her property.

"All I know is her name must start with an M," I say.

Delilah shoves more things into the suitcases. "Don't worry about it or her. There's nothing you can do about either of them."

I throw my hands in the air. "How can you say that? It was clear she was running from something or someone. There was pure fear in her eyes. I've never seen that look in anyone I know. It doesn't make me feel right, not trying to find out what happened to her or if she needs help."

Delilah stops. "So don't give up. Keep your distance and track the fence lines daily. If M is there, she'll eventually come out again. You have to be respectful and not stalkerish."

"Okay, that sounds like a good plan. You'll be hearing from me with whatever I find out, just so you know." I grin.

"I wouldn't expect anything less." She goes back to packing. "Can you believe I'm engaged to Sebastian King? I still can't wrap my head around it."

"Gag, no thanks to the commitment. It scares the living heck out of me. I'm happy living at home and wooing ladies too much. I've got it good here."

She stops and gives me a deadpan look.

"What?"

"Why are you so interested in that girl *M*?" She accentuates the M.

"Because I want to know she's okay," I snap.

"Yeah, yeah," she responds dryly. "I've got to finish packing. I want to say thanks for being my constant lately. From the moment I came home, you had my back. I couldn't ask for a better younger brother."

"I may be younger, but I'm still taller than you."

"Shut up."

"Ready to go?" Sebastian stands in the doorway.

Delilah's face lights up, and I know this is right for her. She zips up her suitcases and faces him. "Yep." They grab the bags and walk out the door.

I follow, so I can say goodbye.

I can't see myself falling hard like that. Nope, no way. People get hurt. I've seen it too many times, and no girl wants to live on a ranch, which again makes the idea of commitment another hard pass for me. Besides, city girls are all about clothes, money, and nightclubs.

Maybe one day I'll settle down, but that day's not here yet. This bachelor is one happy cowboy, and right now, I'm going to get Buster and run the fence line.

Purely to check she's okay, of course.

There's absolutely no other reason.

The End

Thank you so much for reading Delilah and Sebastian's story.

*Turn the page for a look at **The One to Protect** which is Harley and Mysterious M's story. Order your copy: books2read.com/u/4X6Vya*

To keep up to date with what's happening, sign up for my Newsletter: app.mailerlite.com/webforms/landing/w4c9g7

*Or join my reader group **Lovelock's Flock:** facebook.com/groups/742675105787263*

Preview The One to Protect

(Rose Ridge Ranch Book 2)

Chapter One

Mirella

When people talk about their life being turned upside down, flipped sideways, or doing a complete 360, I've always thought that it's not as bad as what they're making it out to be. Not anymore. My life has been flipped upside down, chopped into tiny insignificant pieces, and put through a blender. The people I thought cared for and loved me are not who they seemed to be. They're those kinds of people who wear masks to hide their real identities. I couldn't be who they wanted me to be. Marry who they wanted me to marry. So, I left. Runaway.

They say blood is thicker than water, but in my situation that's not the case. My family only saw the dollar signs my future husband brought to the family and our business, nothing of how I felt about it. Now I'm in a place I never planned to be. After a month here I've decided ranch life isn't my cup of tea. Heck, I don't even drink tea. Gross. I'm not built for the work that goes on around here. Give me a rooftop party and lots of alcohol, along with some close friends, and I've got myself a good time. Not shoveling manure from a stall. I gag at the thought.

I needed out, away from my family, and the only way I could do that was with the help of Carson who arranged Dotty's house for me to stay in. My family and fiancé have the means to find me anywhere, but they won't find me here. I want time to figure out who I am. Who is Mirella? What do I want out of my life apart from becoming a high tea planner and stay-at-home mom? After watching my mother be that doting wife, I realized long ago that I couldn't do it. *Won't do it*, sounds more like me.

A boisterous knock at the old, paint-chipped wooden door startles me as I lay in bed with the covers over my head, attempting to console myself with the choices I've made. "You have some jobs to do around the ranch, girl." The old lady who runs the ranch, Dotty, bellows through the closed door. I roll my eyes. This has been my life for the last month, I've kind of lost track of time, and since my stint with the mustang it's like she's punishing me for drawing attention to myself and her. The way she scowled at the neighbor when he dropped me home, wow, if looks could kill, I'd probably be made to dig the hole and bury the body.

"Okay," I call back. "Be down shortly." Though I'll move like a turtle to not have to shovel out the horse stalls again. Hiding away for a while was my choice. Where I came from, I was the princess of the family and didn't have to do this kind of work.

Knowing Dotty, if I'm not downstairs within the next ten minutes she'll be back upstairs, and this time, she won't be as polite, not that I'd call her polite. She's rough, tough even, and takes no crap from anyone, especially the guy from next door. Harley, I think his name is. My mind flashes back to when I first arrived and the time he saved me from the wild, crazy horse that had a mind of its own. It's a beautiful animal, but for my first time on one it probably wasn't the smartest idea I've ever had, and since then I've not gone near it.

Flicking the blanket back, I sit upright, my double bed creaking with the movement, and swing my legs over the side. My body aches in places that not even my personal trainer has ever gotten to hurt. Standing, I move to the large window. From time to time I'll catch Dotty trying to work with the crazy horse, but it won't have anything to do with her. It's in the round pen already. I guess she plans to work with the horse today. Perhaps I should learn its name instead of calling it horse.

Harley has come to the house a few times, and I've heard him ask about me, but Dotty always tells him to keep his nose out of other people's business. I'm sure she's just doing her job in keeping me safe but it's so boring. I'm actually surprised he's still coming and checking up on me because I was so rude to him. My embarrassment was in overdrive that day and anger was and always is my first response. Whenever someone comes to the ranch I usually just stay out of sight, it's easier than trying to explain who I am. I bought a new phone before leaving, and so thankfully, I can still contact those who are my true friends and were on my side when I chose to leave, they helped me pack.

I bend over and slide on my black runners. They really aren't black anymore since they're coated in mud and who knows what else. I grab a long-sleeved pink button-up shirt and tug it over my white crop top and pull my long hair into a messy bun.

With a sigh, I twist the tight, slightly rusted doorknob and head along a small hallway and down the stairs. This house could be one for the antique community. Thankfully Dotty has updated kitchen appliances which include a coffee machine. Coming down the stairs, I turn to another small hallway and head through a swinging door where the scent of coffee tickles my sense.

A dark green travel mug sits on the grey stone counter, the same one she's left out for me every morning as if she knows my routine. When I glance around, the room is empty. The four-seater wooden table is neat and tidy as if no one has sat at it. Curtains and windows are open with the fresh air gently blowing through them. It's a rather open space but not vast for a large group of people.

Dotty prides herself in her home and in her animals, but she struggles with the rest of the large property. She's not as young as she once was like I've seen in her pictures in the hallways. It baffles me how someone her age has managed this place alone. Though there is one wedding photo in the hallway, it doesn't look like her. I've been too scared to ask her about it because she seems so closed off and doesn't like sharing things about her personal life.

Sometimes at night we'll be sitting in the living room, her in her old black leather recliner, her legs curled up under her with a novel in her hand, and I'll be watching something on the small television — at least it's color. There will be a moment of silence and I'll ask a question, like if she has any kids, and she'll put her book down and stare at me as though she's peering into my soul. Without a word she'll go back to her book, clearly, she doesn't like talking about herself. I guess it's fair enough since I am a complete stranger.

Collecting the mug off the counter, I pull the lid off and check the contents, it looks like coffee that I'd make myself. Dotty is clearly perceptive of things like how I have my coffee in the morning. Pressing the lid back on, I head out the back door and down the few stairs before my shoes crunch on the dirt. Here we go, another day of boring jobs that I absolutely hate. I need something other than my normal though. My happiness was nothing to those closest to me, but I can't live that life anymore. Now it's my turn to learn and thrive in a different way.

Grab your copy of **The One to Protect**
(Rose Ridge Ranch, #2)
books2read.com/u/4X6Vya

To keep up to date with what's happening, sign up for my Newsletter:
app.mailerlite.com/webforms/landing/w4c9g7

Or join my reader group **Lovelock's Flock:**
facebook.com/groups/742675105787263

Other Books by Liz Lovelock

Lost Series
The Lost One — Book One
The Missing One — Book Two
Lost Series Boxed Set

Letters in Blood Series
Dear Captor — Book One
With Love — Book Two
Forever Yours — Book Three
Dear Captor Boxed Set

My Guy Series
Monday Night Guy — Book One
My Aussie Guy — Book Two
My Forbidden Guy — Book Three
The Right Guy — Book Four
My Guy Series Complete Boxed Set

The Jilted Series
Something Old — Book One
Something New — Book Two
Something Borrowed — Book Three
Something Blue — Book Four
Something Beautiful — Book Five — A Novella

Rose Ridge Ranch Series
The One to Heal — Book One
The One to Protect — Book Two

Acknowledgements

I'll say sorry first in case I miss anyone. The One to Heal was such an amazing story to write. I love these characters and love what their future books will be like.

I'd like to thank all those who helped get The One to Heal in tip top shape—Lauren from Creating Ink, Kaylene, Chantell and Nikki from Swish Design & Editing and Lisa Vincent. Without you ladies, I'd be thoroughly lost. You've all pushed me with this one. You're awesome! Thanks for all your advice and guidance.

A huge thank you to Ben from Tall Story for designing the perfect cover. It is everything I wanted it to be. I love it!

These next mentions are my other halves in the author world. Without their constant support and friendship, I may have given up a long time ago. They're my cyber sisters spread far and wide around Australia and America, so thank you to

Jemma Brown aka JB Heller, Kaylene Osborn, and Belle Brooks. These ladies are truly amazing. I'd be lost without our chats.

Huge shout out to my awesome Beta Readers who offered heaps of support and encouragement. Thank you Donna, Anastasia, Halle, Margaret, Sheena, Tracey and Vicki.

To my Flock—I love you, girls. Your support is truly nothing short of amazing. I know I have a safe place in my group with you all. Thank you.

To my readers—I feel blessed to have your continuous support. Thank you.

To my family and my husband—you're truly wonderful. You've never given up on me. You sit and listen when I need to vent out my frustrations, never once complaining about it. I love you.

To my three beautiful children—Millie, Cale, and Finn. You three test my patience, but I'm so grateful to have you in my life to love. Families are forever.

About the Author

I'm a wife, mother, reader, blogger, and now an author. I'm always busy doing something as I have so much going on, and my three little ones keep me on my toes.

I'm from bright and sunny Queensland, Australia. I have always been a reader. When I was little, I would be up late reading *Garfield* and *Asterix* comic books and also *Footrot Flats*. When I hit high school, they gave us *Tomorrow When the War Began* by John Marsden, and from there my love of books continued to grow.

I keep a notebook and pen beside my bed for when those late-night ideas pop into my head, plus I'm a stationery addict and love pens, notebooks, and, well, anything stationery.

Connect with Liz Online

Check these links for more information about author Liz Lovelock.

TikTok ~ tiktok.com/@lizlovelockauthor
Twitter ~ @LizLovelock
Email ~ lizlovelockauthor@gmail.com
Website ~ lizlovelockauthor.com/
Facebook ~ facebook.com/people/Liz-Lovelock-Author/100008389321975/
Goodreads ~ goodreads.com/author/show/8268717.Liz_Lovelock
Instagram ~ instagram.com/lizlovelock/

Or sign up for my **Newsletter**:
app.mailerlite.com/webforms/landing/w4c9g7